"**K**ill confirmed," sa[...] you're clear to adv[...]

"Alright damn it, move, move, move," the Marine Captain relayed over the radio, advancing his men into action. Buck slammed another round into the chamber and lined up a shot at a terrorist wielding an AK-47 in the window of the house (according to the higher-ups, it was a mini-fortress). The soldier shuddered as the bullet penetrated his right eye, killing the tribesman stone-dead instantly.

Buck chambered another round and surveyed the compound. The squad of marines was advancing on the east side of the property, while Buck and his spotter were on the north side. A group of seventeen terrorists armed to the teeth with assault rifles, LMG's, (light machine guns) and RPG's(rocket propelled grenade) swarmed out of the compound, threatening to overwhelm the small unit of Marines. Buck gritted his teeth. *Once again, command fucked up. "We only expect minimal resistance" my ass.*

LIGHTNING STRIKES TWICE

WILLIAM H. LaBARGE

A GORDIAN KNOT MILITARY THRILLER

Best Wishes
"Sweetwater"
Jim Boyze

In Remembrance of:
Captain Conrad "WarBucks" Langley, Jr. (Ret.)

CHAPTER ONE

THE IDES OF MARCH

February 20, 2013

President Irene Fletcher sat at her desk in the Oval Office, rapping her fingers against the arms of her black leather chair, idly wasting time until her next meeting. She was facing the window outside, and she watched the city of Washington D.C. bustle through the cold February morning. Her quiet moment was interrupted by her administrative assistant, Ms. Susan Clukey.

"Mrs. President?" The redhead quietly knocked on the door as she opened it.

Irene turned around in her chair to face Susan. "Yes dear? Is there something I can help you with?"

"The Director of the CIA and the Secretary of Defense are urgently requesting to see you, ma'am. They say it's important. Do you want me to let them in?"

The president cleared her desk and motioned with her hand. "Yes of course, let them in."

Irene stood up and prepared to greet her guests. The sixty-three-year-old President of the United States was wearing a navy blue two-piece tweed suit with a white-ruffled front, long sleeve blouse. A pearl necklace was draped across her neck, and she was wearing nude shear nylons with glossy black heels. Supporters and opponents of Mrs. Fletcher called her a cross between Queen Elizabeth and Ronald Reagan, and they couldn't be more right. She had a warm, friendly smile, but leaders around the world knew better than to mistake her kindness for weakness. She was an excellent strategist, calm and collected, but she was also a sleeping dragon—anger her, and you would absolutely regret it. Above all though, she loved her country and her allies. It didn't take long for America and the rest of the world to fall in love with her.

Moments later, the door opened again, and two well-dressed gentlemen rushed into the room, a look of worry on their faces. Lyle "Ho Chi" Bien, the Director of the CIA and Larry Blumberg, the Secretary of Defense, entered the Oval Office. Both men looked tired; their suits were wrinkled and their hair disheveled. Director Bien, with a concerned look on his face, skipped the pleasantries and jumped right in.

"Mrs. President, something has come up." The boyish smile that normally graced his face was nowhere to be seen.

Irene motioned for them to sit down, and she took her seat.

"Well, what is it? From the look on your faces, I'm liable to think Hitler himself has come back from the dead."

The Secretary of Defense pulled a grey laptop out of his briefcase, opened it and turned it to Irene. On the screen was a picture of a power plant set beside a river. It was surrounded by what looked to be farmland, which in turn was surrounded by a large city.

While Irene was putting on her glasses to look at the laptop, the Secretary of Defense asked, "Do you know of the Bushehr Power Plant? It's a Russian-built nuclear plant that has been essentially dormant since the 1990's."

The president studied the screen, and then looked up at Larry. "Well yes, I have been briefed on it. Like you said though, it's been dormant for years. What of it?"

Director Bien interjected, "It *was* dormant. We received word through PRISM that it came online two days ago."

Irene took off her glasses and leaned back into her chair. Director Bien continued, "Iran has always wanted to become a nuclear power, but they have never had the resources, or frankly the balls to actually do anything about it. Until now, at least."

At that moment, there was a quick knock at the door before it opened. General Black "Jack" Sealock, Director of the NSA, (National Security Agency) walked briskly into the room holding a brown leather-bound folder.

"Apologies for being late," he mumbled, running his fingers through his wind-blown gray hair as his free hand rummaged through the folder. When he found what he was looking for, he lifted out several documents and set them on the president's desk.

"I'm sure by now they've told you of the Bushehr Power Plant. I'm afraid our problems don't end there."

Irene put her glasses back on and looked at the documents, which mostly consisted of pictures of a specific plane, labeled Flight IA 0000.

"We've been tracking this very plane for the past two

months now. It's a bimonthly flight that originates in Iran and flies to Caracas, Venezuela, while making stops in Beirut and Damascus." Sealock ran his hands through his hair again and scratched the back of his neck before he continued, "The plane always uses the same flight path, on the same days, just like clockwork. The strange thing is that even though it lands at public airports, it never passes through any kind of immigration or customs. Once the plane lands in Caracas, it taxies to a hanger, shuts down its engines and is towed inside, with the doors closing behind it. Nothing comes in or out for two days that we can visibly see. After that, the hangar doors open, the plane is towed out, the engines are started, and the plane taxies to the active runway and takes off."

"This plane, 'Flight IA 0000' has been an absolute mystery for the past two months, a brain teaser that, quite frankly, I thought never really had an answer. That is, until the Bushehr Power Plant came back online."

Gen. Sealock paused before he continued, "The flight originates from the Bushehr airport. Now, we still have no idea who or what is on this plane, but I know one thing for certain: whatever it is, it has something to do with that nuclear power plant. The question is, what is it, and what do we do about it?"

No one had an answer. The chilling cold that permeated the Washington D.C. landscape was nothing compared to the chilling fear that gripped President Irene Fletcher's heart. The silence that permeated the room was deafening. Four of the most powerful people in the world sat drowning in this silence, unable to answer the question. All of their minds drifted to the worst possible conclusions, and the realization that their worst night-mares could be real possibilities was not lost on them.

President Fletcher slowly took off her glasses, leaned back into her chair and whispered, "Godammit". Taking a deep breath, she looked at the three men in front of her. "This is disturbing news" she uttered, although desperate for more answers, there were none at this time. "Gentlemen, by midafternoon I want a report on my desk substantiating what we've discussed here this morning. I'll have a message to you all by six; you're excused."

As the three exited the Oval Office, they walked to the room's other door, which led to a hidden staircase. Irene buzzed Ms. Clukey into the office. When she entered, the president told her to cancel the rest of her morning meetings and that she wasn't to be disturbed. "Yes Ma'am" Ms. Clukey replied, and she hurriedly left the Oval Office, closing the door behind her.

Irene sat down and penned one of the most important messages she had ever written in her short tenure as the Leader of the Free World. She recapped the events that had just been brought to her attention to Admiral Tim LaFleur, the Chief of Naval Operations (CNO), and up the chain of command at the pentagon, closing with the statement, "It's time to bring in the best."

CHAPTER TWO
WETTING-A-LINE

February 2013

Lieutenant Zac Taylor studied his friend's face before saying, "You're bluffing."

Lieutenant Howard Sullivan flashed a smile, responding with, "Am I? With the way you play poker, I wouldn't be so sure of that. Either way, you gotta make a decision—are you going to fold? We've been at this for hours."

"Hell no I'm not folding! You owe me at least 16 beers goddammit, and I'm going to get it out of you one way or the other." With that, Zac pushed all of his chips into the center of the table. "All in, Sully."

Sullivan grunted, "I hate it when you call me that."

"That's pretty much the only reason why I call you that."

Howard threw all of his chips into the center as well. "Remind me why I don't kick your ass all the time?"

Zac flipped over his cards—three tens and two sixes stared back up at him. "You don't kick my ass because you owe me money. Full House! I'll accept payment in cash or beer—your choice."

Howard sighed. "No Zac, that's not why I don't kick your ass—" he paused to flip over his cards. "I don't kick your ass because it is *you* who owes me money." Zac couldn't believe the Royal Flush that made up Howard's cards.

"You sonofabitch! I swear to God you're cheating somehow, I just don't know how."

Zac's tirade was cut short by a loud, thunderous boom.

Howard quickly got up. "What the hell? That sounded like an explosion." Several more explosions filled the air before the air raid sirens went off.

Howard quickly reached for his coat. "Ah fuck! Zac, grab your jacket, we gotta go!"

Howard opened the door to the outside and was greeted by fire, death, and shrapnel. Both men stood dumbfounded as they observed the pandemonium before them. A low-flying plane screamed by to strafe the barracks next door, bringing them back to reality.

"Sully, did you see that? Th-that plane—it was Japanese! Holy fuck."

Howard nodded his head, trying to figure out what to do next. Out of the corner of his eye he spotted an undamaged jeep. "Zac! The jeep! That's our ride to the airstrip. Hopefully there will be some aircraft left so we can get into the fight."

The two men rushed to the jeep. "Sully, you drive!" Zac yelled as he jumped into the passenger seat. Before Howard could climb into the jeep, an explosion knocked him off his feet. "Ah shit! The *Arizona*! They hit the *Arizona*!"

Howard climbed back up to his feet and paused to look

at the carnage. In that instant time slowed and the sound of the battle around him muffled as he watched the USS *Arizona* begin to list and slowly break in half. The screams of the dying and wounded slowly brought him back.

"Howard! Howard? Godammit Sully, we gotta go!"

"Right, uh, shit. I'm on it."

Luckily, the keys were already in the ignition. Howard fired up the jeep and began to race towards the airfield, dodging rubble, debris, and falling aircraft. He was focused on the road until he heard Zac.

"Uh, Sully? You should probably start driving faster."

"What?" asked Howard, unable to understand what Zac was saying.

"You might want to drive faster!"

"What?"

"DRIVE FASTER THERE'S A FUCKING ZERO BEHIND US!"

Howard looked behind him and saw the white-painted Japanese Zero barreling down on them. The aircraft began to light up the road with machine gun fire. Howard began swerving from left to right, frantically dodging the machine gun fire. Up ahead, there was a dirt path through some woods that led directly to the airfield.

"Hang on Zac! It's gonna get bumpy!" Howard cut a quick left and blasted into the woods. The enemy Zero, having missed its prey, climbed towards the clouds and continued the attack on the harbor.

The jeep finally made its way to the airfield, and Howard parked it next to one of the hangars.

"Alright Zac, once we're airborne, cover my six. We're going to smoke as many Zekes as we can. And remember, it ain't over 'till the Fat Lady Sings".

The two pilots suited up and got into their P-40 Tomahawks. As they taxied to the runway, Howard spotted a group of aircraft heading their way.

The P-40's accelerated in an attempt to get into the air and maneuver away from the incoming Zeke's. Howard's fighter was airborne first, and he headed for the clouds. Machine gun fire began to pound the pavement right behind Zac's plane.

"Come on baby, come on baby. Faster. Faster. Faster!"

Finally he built up enough speed to get airborne and make a sharp turn over the trees to avoid the attacking Zeros as he climbed above the clouds. For the moment, he was safe. Zac couldn't help but wonder just how peaceful and serene it was up above the clouds. The sun was shining; the clouds themselves looked like soft, white beds that were just asking you to lie on them. It was difficult to believe that below him the worst attack on United States soil was underway.

"Hey Sully, what's your posit?"

Howard radioed back, "Twelve o'clock, four thousand feet."

"Roger, got ya, I'm rolling in on your six." Zac's Tomahawk pulled up behind Howard's.

"Okay big guy, here we go."

Howard put his P-40 Tomahawk into a sharp dive and plunged below the clouds. What he saw below looked like Armageddon. The once beautiful Pearl Harbor was ablaze. Fire was everywhere, ships were sinking, and the sky itself was full of white Zero's. Howard gritted his teeth, locked in on a nearby zeke and went for the kill.

The torpedo plane ahead of him must not have known there were U.S. fighters around, because he took no evasive maneuvers. Howard carefully lined up his shot, and pulled the trigger. Bullets ravaged the plane and tore the left wing in half. The aircraft began to spin out of control, and crashed into the ocean below.

"Not a bad start Sully!" Zac shouted over the combat frequency.

The easy kills were over, however a formation of four Zero's began to hone in on the duo. To avoid them, Howard and Zac climbed back into the clouds, and they both performed a half-Cuban-Eight maneuver and rolled in behind the zekes.

"Let's light 'em up Zac!" The two pilots tore into the Japanese planes, downing three of them. Both cheered as the enemy aircraft crashed into the drink below.

There was no time for celebration, as they had stirred up the hornets' nest. Two four-plane formations rolled in on Howard and Zac. The two pilots began yanking and banking around the enemy planes, carefully choosing when to engage. Zac almost bought the farm when he couldn't shake a Zero off his tail—but luckily Howard had his six covered and smoked the Zero.

"You're welcome!"

Eventually, the numbers began to be too much. Howard and Zac were great pilots, but they weren't superheroes. Zac's plane was hit first.

"Ah fuck! I'm hit!" A flurry of bullets tore into his rudder and his Tomahawk began tumbling out of control. Zac hit the silk before his plane exploded in mid-air.

Howard's plane was on fire, and bullet holes riddled

both the inside and the outside. Blood spurted from his shoulder; shrapnel from his own plane had embedded itself in his arm. Eventually, his plane stopped responding to his commands. As the plane started to cart wheel through the sky, Howard said to himself as he bailed out, it's time to send this aircraft back to the taxpayers. A few seconds later, the canopy popped open and Howard was under a white cloud of safety as his chute drifted down to the ocean. As his feet entered the water, another explosion was set off beside him.

Matt "Sweetwater" Sullivan was awakened by his dog, Boomer, who had jumped on his bed.

"Oh hey there boy! Had that dream about my grandfather again." Boomer looked at him with a doggish smile, and barked. "Yeah, yeah. I know. C'mon, let's get us some breakfast."

As Sweetwater hopped out of bed and walked to the kitchen to prepare breakfast, he thought about his grandfather. Howard must have told him that story hundreds of times, but it always enthralled Matt. In fact, it was those stories that convinced him to become a fighter pilot himself.

Howard Sullivan survived the attack on Pearl Harbor, and eventually went on to kick ass all around the Pacific Rim.

"What about Zac, grandpa? What happened to him? Did he make it?" Matt would always ask.

"Absolutely. That sonofabitch refused to die. He never did pay me for that night of poker. Which, by the way, I'll collect one day."

Matt had just finished his tour as Commanding Officer of the "Screaming Eagles" VFA-51, which was deployed to the Western Pacific on the *USS Enterprise* (CVN-65) for eight months. After his Change-of-Command in August of 2012, Commander Sullivan reported to Naval Air Force, U.S. Pacific Fleet as the Fighter Training Officer. In February 2013, he was promoted to Captain and assumed Command of Carrier Air Wing Eleven.

It had been over fifteen months since Matt had requested leave. Therefore, he decided to take a break and get his battery charged before taking command of Airwing Eleven. It was time to pack his fishing gear, load up Boomer and head up to his mountain cabin to do a little trout fishing.

After man and beast finished their breakfast, they were restless to start the day.

"Alright Boomer. We're on vacation! What do you want to do?"

Boomer barked.

"Hell yeah. Fishing it is!"

Matt loved going up to Mammoth Lakes, located in central California. He owned a small log cabin outside of town, where he spent most of his time fly-fishing, hunting, skiing and hanging out at the local watering hole.

After a full day of fly-fishing, Boomer and Matt had caught more fish than they could eat. Once the fish were cleaned and put in the freezer, Matt cleaned up and decided to have a few snaps at the Mangy Moose, a bar he always visited. Before leaving, Matt got a roaring blaze going in his fieldstone fireplace, so Boomer would have a warm place to curl up and sleep. He walked out the front door wearing a black fleece jacket, blue jeans, and a pair of black cowboy boots. Being a well-built, 6'2", tan forty-seven-year-old with steely hazel eyes, people couldn't deny one thing when they saw him; he looked good.

As he walked inside the bar, he was reminded why he loved this place. The bartender knew his favorite drink, the men were friendly and the women were beautiful. He could feel two of those women's eyes on him, a blonde and a brunette, as he ordered his Scotch on the rocks. Torch, who, in his opinion, was one of the sexiest bartenders west of the Mississippi, had fixed his drinks for the last twelve years at the Moose. Sweetwater wasted no time. He had never needed the liquid courage to talk to beautiful women. He walked over to the table.

"Good evening ladies. Name's Matt. Care if I join you?" His eyes were fixed on the brunette.

The brunette spoke up first, "Well Matt, absolutely you can. I'm Mary Farrio, and this . . ." she poked the blonde, ". . . is Amy Greene."

Matt nodded at the ladies and said, "It's a pleasure to meet you, Mary. And you as well, Amy. Can I buy you two some drinks?"

"Sure, we're both drinking Merlot," Mary said, smiling at Matt.

Matt went to the bar and ordered for them. While he was waiting for Torch to pour their wine, he asked her if she'd seen these gals in there before.

"No sir, I've never seen them until a few nights ago."

"Thanks Torch, you're as hot as ever!" Torch laughed as Matt walked back to the table.

Matt returned to the table with their drinks, continued

with the small chatter and waited for the obvious question.

"What do you do Matt," Mary asked.

Matt rolled up his sleeves and smiled. "Well, I own a woman's design salon in La Jolla."

"Oh really?" Mary took a sip of her wine. "What exactly do you sell?"

"Well, it's more of a service. You see, I shave women's legs, perform bikini cuts and do design work as requested." Matt looked at them with a straight, serious face.

Mary looked at Amy, and they both burst out in laughter.

Mary said, "You've got to be shitting me!"

"No ma'am, my establishment is called "Sweetwater's International Leg Shaving and Sensitivity Salon. I've shaved several thousand sets of legs without a cut or scratch. It's my greatest talent."

"Bullshit" Amy says. "I cut myself just about every time I shave."

Matt laughed, "Well, you obviously need to set up an appointment and have it done right! It's all about the angles, Amy."

At that moment, a gentleman interrupted and asked Amy to dance, which she agreed to. As she held out her hand and was escorted to the dance floor, she looked over at Matt and just shook her head.

After Amy was clear from behind the table, Mary asked "So, Matt, what's this 'Sweetwater' all about?"

"Oh, that's my nickname."

"Nickname? Hmm. And how did you receive that moniker?" Mary asked.

"Well, after college I played a season of Minor League

baseball and I got tagged with that call sign due to the cologne I wore while playing. My teammates called me 'Sweetwater Willie, from North South Philly."

Mary laughed. "You know what, Sweetwater? You're more full of shit than a bird cage."

Matt flashed a smile. "Well, I can't argue with you there!" Taking a swig of his scotch, he asked, "So what do you do Ms. Mary?"

"I'm a surgeon at Scripps Green hospital in La Jolla."

"Wow, that sounds exciting. What do you specialize in?"

"Design Work."

Matt began to really feel for this girl. He decided to tell her what he really did. "All right. You got me. I'm actually the Commanding Officer for Air Wing Eleven, aboard the *USS Ronald Reagan*, (CVN-76)."

Mary jumped in, "I knew that haircut had something to do with your job! Now, what about this leg shaving gig?"

Matt smiled, "Mary, that is a long story. When we have more time, I'll explain the whole gig to you. How about a dance?"

"I'd love to." Mary replied.

The couple danced to a few songs, and they talked about everything, work, their childhood, friends, loves, and each other. Eventually, the conversation wound down to a single question: "Want to head back down to my place?" Sweetwater asked.

Mary looked up at him with her brown eyes, "I'd love that."

They didn't even make it to Matt's front door before they started kissing. The passion was so intense that Matt had to breathe, "We have to do this inside." Mary laughed, and they both stumbled inside. Boomer looked up when he saw them enter the living room, and laid his head back down, close to the warm fireplace.

Mary threw Sweetwater down on the couch and began to take her shirt off. She tossed it on the floor when Sweetwater's cell phone rang.

Matt groaned. "Oh no."

Mary grinned, putting her thumb against her mouth. "It's okay. I know you're a superhero already. Go ahead, answer it!"

"I'm sorry; I need to take this call." Matt grabbed the phone and put it up to his ear. "Sweetwater here."

"CAG, this is Vice Admiral Balmert. Son, I'm going to have to cut your leave short." Admiral Balmert was the head of 3rd Fleet and was responsible for the training of Naval Forces for overseas deployments. He also evaluated the state of the art technology for fleet use.

"Sir?"

"Matt, I hate to do this, but I can't tell you anymore. All I can say is that we need you in my office at 0700 tomorrow morning. We'll be able to tell you more then."

"Yes Sir." Matt said firmly, "I'll see you in the morning," as he closed his cell phone. He knew in order to make that deadline he'd have to leave immediately.

He slowly turned around and told Mary that he needed to return to San Diego.

Mary's flirty smile immediately changed to sadness. "I guess you can't tell me why, can you?"

Matt shook his head. "I can't tell you because I don't even know. I just have to be in San Diego in six hours."

He walked over, grabbed her hands and kissed her on the cheek. "I promise you, I am going to call, this isn't a one night stand. I'm not going to let you go that easily. You got it?"

Mary smiled, "Got it."

Sweetwater quickly packed his things, threw on a pair of sweats, grabbed Boomer and headed for San Diego. Even though Vice Admiral Balmert hadn't said anything in his cryptic phone call, Matt was sure of one thing: shit was about to hit the fan.

CHAPTER THREE

THE SLEEPING DOG IS AWAKENED

"Alright Buck, ballistics look good, take the shot when you're ready."

Gunnery Sergeant Buck Cassidy peered through the scope of his .50 cal sniper rifle, adjusted for distance and wind, and then fired. With a crack like thunder, the bullet sped out of the barrel of his gun. A second later, his shot found its target, an Al Qaeda sentry. The bullet entered and exited his skull, and the sentry dropped like a rock.

"Kill confirmed," said Milo, Buck's spotter. "Captain, you're clear to advance. We'll keep you covered."

"Alright damn it, move, move, move," the Marine Captain relayed over the radio, advancing his men into action. Buck slammed another round into the chamber and lined up a shot at a terrorist wielding an AK-47 in the window of the house (according to the higher-ups, it was a mini-fortress). The soldier shuddered as the bullet penetrated his right eye, killing the tribesman stone-dead instantly.

Buck chambered another round and surveyed the compound. The squad of marines was advancing on the east side of the property, while Buck and his spotter were on the north side. A group of seventeen terrorists armed to the teeth with assault rifles, LMG's, (light machine guns) and RPG's(rocket propelled grenade) swarmed out of the compound, threatening to overwhelm the small unit of Marines. Buck gritted his teeth. *Once again, command fucked up. "We only expect minimal resistance" my ass.*

"Get down!" Milo yelled, and Buck pulled his head down as a rocket propelled grenade slammed into the ground beside him.

"Ah shit Buck, they're on to us," his spotter yelled, his ears still ringing from the blast of the grenade. Buck could hear the Marine Captain yelling over the radio, frantically trying to get his men into position.

"I know, calm down, I've got these assholes between my crosshairs." Buck said coolly.

He lined his sights on the forehead of the terrorist who was wielding the RPG. As he peered through his scope and started to squeeze the trigger, he got a better idea. He moved the crosshairs to the rocket itself, and slowly compressed the trigger. A second later, the rocket blew up in the hostile's hands, killing him and three others around him.

"Damn, nice shot," his spotter said.

At that point Buck could hear the Marine Captain shouting orders. "Nerenberg, cover Jenkins' six! Don't give them a goddamn inch!"

Right at that moment, the door to the compound opened, and out stepped a bearded man wearing a kameez dress and a karakul hat, indicating he was an elder. He calmly walked out to the firefight, and brandished what looked to be a 9 millimeter pistol. He began waving it around, barking orders to the tribesman defending the house. The man paused for a moment, and then looked north. He looked right at Buck.

Buck's heart stopped. *He had seen this man before.*

Two years ago, Cassidy was on a search and destroy mission near Feyzabad. His target was an Al Qaeda General, Mohammad Hashim, who was a ruthless military leader whose hit squad frequently murdered the military and the civilian aide that was trying to help the citizens of Afghanistan.

Mohammad Hashim eked out a living in the northeast section of Afghanistan, near the border of Tajikistan. When CIA intelligence managed to spot him directly north of Feyzabad, Buck was ordered to send him a present. The mountainous terrain would have made any kind of preparation difficult for a normal sniper, but Gunny Buck was not a normal sniper. He took minimal supplies so as not to load himself down. It was difficult in itself to become acclimated working at this elevation. In order to get a clear shot, Buck climbed 3,300 feet up the Hindu Kush, and lay atop a peak for over two days. His situational awareness had started to diminish, but he laid there as still and silent as death itself.

Finally, his target came into view. The General and his entourage were taking a small break from driving. They were all standing outside their vehicle, stretching their legs and having a smoke. The General and one other man broke off from the group and began to walk down a trail. This was Buck Cassidy's moment. He had prepared for days awaiting this kill shot. He licked his chapped lips, his sniper rifle was cocked and loaded and he slowed his breathing for the shot. It felt like eternity had passed as he squeezed the trigger. For five seconds, nothing happened, then the bullet ripped into Mohammad Hashim's skull, and the impact threw him backwards. The man beside him rushed to his leader's side, but he knew it was over. Buck chambered another round and prepared to fire. His crosshairs lined up on the man's face, which looked up directly at Buck, almost as though he was staring into his soul.

"Gunny you need to get out of there now. The Al Qaeda are climbing out of the woodwork. You've worn out your welcome, son." His CO was on the other end of the radio, watching the mission via a nearby UAV.

Buck tripped his safety on, and started down the mountain.

Other snipers have analyzed the shot that Gunny Buck Cassidy made that day, and they called it one of the most difficult kill-shots ever. An official report was filed substantiating that Gunnery Sergeant Buck Cassidy's shot had the precision which equated to shooting an arrow through the keyhole of a train moving 60 mph, which is how he earned his nickname, "Savage". As a result of that shot, the Taliban put a two million dollar reward on Buck's head for anyone who brought him in—dead or alive.

Buck never thought he'd see that face again, yet here it was, staring up at him from the abyss. Before Buck could get a shot off, the man slid into cover, out of sight.

"I had him in my crosshairs, but couldn't get the shot off. Captain, can your guys flush him out for me?" Buck asked over the radio.

"A little busy over here! You give us some cover, and

we'll do the flushing!" the Captain snapped back.

"Roger that, sir." Buck turned his attention to the Taliban firing at the Marines, and quickly whittled their numbers.

After several of them dropped like flies, the terrorists started to break ranks and fall back to the house itself. The Marine Captain bellowed over the radio, "Here comes your flush!"

Buck watched through his scope as the Captain threw a grenade close to where the man had taken cover. Buck lined up his shot and waited. The man rushed out of cover like a cheetah, and sped towards the door. He was moving in a serpentine motion, and at that distance, Buck was concerned with the accuracy of his shot. Because the temperature was 10 to15 degrees warmer than this morning, Buck knew he had to drop his sights down a half inch or so to compensate for muzzle velocity. The sight pictures didn't feel right but his gut relied on his training. He squeezed the trigger, BAM!

Smoke cleared from Buck's rifle as he awaited confirmation. A second later, the bullet had torn into the man's chest, leaving a hole the size of a fist where his heart used to be.

"Shot through the heart, Savage. Kill confirmed," replied his spotter.

With the death of their leader, the rest of the tribesman quickly surrendered.

"Not a bad day, gentlemen. Buck, thanks for joining the dance. You ready to head back?"

As Gunny stepped off the Chinook, he was looking forward

to a hot meal and shower. His dreams were dashed when a young sergeant approached him. Without saying a word, he handed him an envelope, and then stood at attention. Buck opened the seal, and pulled out a letter that simply read:

Find a pole Marine. (A term that strikes fear and misery into a sniper candidate, because he must immediately find a desk, chair, a windowsill, or a pole to elevate their feet to commence push-ups.)

Buck groaned. "Where?"

The aide pointed to a nearby tent, and walked off.

Inside the tent was General Robert "MADDOG" Hamer, a 57 year old, buzz-cut white haired, gravelly voice, multi-dimensional thinker who was waiting for Buck to enter. As Gunny Buck entered the tent, the General threw out the formalities and said, "Stand at ease, Marine." Buck folded his hands behind the small of his back. "Son, I hate to rain on your parade, but you're needed back in DC. Pack your shit, Gunny, you're leaving in 45 minutes." The General pulled a folder off his desk which said "CLASSIFIED" in bold red. "Don't open this until you're on the plane back to Washington."

Buck gave a "Yes, sir", came to attention, and began to walk out of the tent.

"Savage."

Buck turned around. "Yes, sir?"

"Good luck, this mission is big and needs to be handled with utmost security, understand?"

"Yes Sir", Buck replied.

Gunny had a 15 hour flight back to Andrew's Air Force Base. After lift-off, he had some chow and fell asleep. Prior to landing at Andrews, he read the contents of the "Classified" folder, and then cleaned up before landing.

Upon landing at the base, Buck was escorted to a conference room that served as an operation center. The space was pretty much empty, except for several men in civilian attire. Before he could get comfortable, a man wearing a jet black suit entered the room, and everyone came to attention.

The man made a bee-line to Buck.

"Gunnery Sergeant Cassidy?"

"Yes sir."

"I'm special agent Nick Carter. I'll be escorting you down to The Raven Rock Complex tomorrow for your compartmented brief. Did you review the folder that General Hamer gave you?"

"Yes sir."

"Excellent. Do you have any questions with what you read?"

"Yes sir. A lot of questions."

Special Agent Carter laughed. "No worries Gunny, everyone else that will be attending the brief is in the same boat. Don't worry, everything will be cleared up by tomorrow."

"Roger that, Sir."

"You look tired, son. I'm going to take you to a secure area. Get some rest. I know you've had a long flight. A driver will pick you up at 07:30 and bring you to the Quarter Deck, then a helo will fly us and others down to the Complex for your 0900 briefing. Understood?"

"Yes sir! Thank you."

"One more thing, Gunny. This meeting? It's huge. Get some rest, you're gonna need it."

CHAPTER FOUR
THE BAGGAGE HANDLER

Simon Bolivar International Airport
Maiquetia, Venezuela
13 miles (21kilometers) from downtown Caracas

As Craig "Bastos" Miller clocked in at 1600 for his twenty-second day as a baggage handler at the Caracas International Airport, he couldn't help but smile to himself; today was his final day on the job.

At forty-seven, the 6'3" CIA agent was no stranger to operations like this. His fair skin, gentle eyes, and receding hairline worked together to give him a gentle demeanor, but don't let that fool you. Underneath the pleasant exterior was a viper who wouldn't think twice about slitting your throat.

Miller walked into the employee lounge and casually made a cup of coffee. A few employees chatted him up with some small talk, to which he responded in fluent Spanish. In his mind, however, he wasn't thinking about the conversation; he was focused on why he was here.

His mission was simple: covertly gather info on Flight IA 0000, find out where it was being sheltered, record its cargo and report back to Langley with his findings. Although he was only there for a short time, Bastos had already accumulated an astounding amount of information. Through his investigations, he knew that the aircraft arrived on the third Monday of each month, landed around 1730, taxied to the newly constructed hangar on the west side of the airport and was towed inside. After several days, the plane was pulled out of the hangar, its engines were started, and it taxied to the active runway and departed.

The airport itself was situated on a peninsula, with the longest runway running north and south. The main terminals were on the east side of the airfield and the hangars, along with the newly constructed one, were on the west side, two hundred yards from the ocean's edge.

Bastos knew he wouldn't be able to arrive unannounced at the hangar the plane was housed in. The armed private guards patrolled the outside perimeter 24/7. Any attempt to infiltrate the area would get him captured or shot. However, he had already covertly set up his disguise, which would allow him to come and go without question.

Once a week, employees from the *Lidotel Dry Cleaners* came to the airport to gather up the security guards' clothes and uniforms. Over the past twenty-two days, Bastos had been busy confiscating the security guards' clothing and uniforms directly from the *Lidotel Dry Cleaners*. The security guards reasoned it as incompetence by the dry cleaners, and Bastos got a full uniform out of it. He had also managed to replicate a phony security card, and he had been able to copy various security keys.

Miller glanced at his watch, it was 1800. *"Show time."*

He thought to himself, as he suited up in his security uniform. Once his disguise was on, he extracted his duffle bag with his covert gear and headed for one of the airfield's security cars outside the building.

As he approached the car, he looked across the airfield's runways and saw Flight IA 0000 being towed into the hangar. For the past two weeks, he had made several visits to the new hangar, bringing coffee and donuts to the private guards, using the opportunity to survey the set-up outside the grounds. The guards knew him as "the donut guy" and eagerly awaited his arrival every night.

Around 1830, he arrived with coffee and donuts as he had done several nights earlier. The guards recognized him and eagerly gathered around his security car. As they voraciously dove into the donuts, Agent Miller grabbed a spare donut box, and motioned to the inside of the hangar. He always went inside to give the guard in the hangar itself donuts as well. The guards outside were too busy eating to notice, so Bastos slipped out from the car and walked towards the hangar.

Miller knocked on the side door and a guard peered through the peep hole. Once he recognized who it was, he smiled and unlatched the door, greeting Bastos and his donuts. Bastos started to enter the hangar, just like he had always done, but the guard held his hand up, pointed to the occupied hangar and indicated he couldn't enter. Bastos could see the huge plane chocked in the hangar, then backed away indicating he understood he wasn't allowed in.

He smiled, passed the tray of coffee and donuts to the guard and started to back down. The guard graciously nodded and began to close the door, but before he shut the door, Miller pulled out a stiletto knife from his back pocket and drove it into the guard's jugular vein, killing him instantly. As he slumped to the concrete hangar floor, Bastos grabbed the backpack that he'd laid next to the door before entering and pulled out a bottle of STYPTIC anti-hemorrhagic powder and sealed the injured area. With no blood on the floor, Bastos cleaned up the spilled coffee and pulled the lifeless body of the guard up to and into the right wheel-well of the aircraft, disposing of the body. By doing this, it would allow the gear to retract after takeoff and when the gear was lowered for landing, the airflow would suck the body out the wheel well.

Agent Miller now had to work rapidly and gather the intelligence he'd been sent to extract. He opened the cargo bays and took pictures of Ak-47s, boxes of grenades and other items of interest. It wasn't until he opened the forward pressurized bay and found what he was looking for, that he realized he had hit paydirt. Stacked on top of each other, were a dozen or so elongated silver suitcases which looked like luggage containers.

He grabbed his handheld Geiger Counter and confirmed that there was enriched uranium located in those containers. With this information in hand, his job was completed, so he evacuated the hangar and left by the side door. Nightfall had settled in and the guards had returned to their patrols, so he returned to his car unmolested and threw his backpack in the passenger seat.

As he started to pull out, he saw the security guards walking along the western perimeter. He merely waved at them, and they waved back, none-the-wiser that he had just killed one of their comrades and discovered the contents of Flight IA 0000. As he drove past them, he laughed to himself, saying, "*You dumb shits.*"

Bastos looked at his watch; it was 1905. His extraction time was at 1930, so he knew that he had to hurry to reach his pick-up point. In order to exit the airport without suspicion, he radioed the airport tower and mentioned a possible security breach at the northwest corner of the main runway. He was cleared to investigate, so no one batted an eye when he drove over to the edge of the runway. He got out of his vehicle, checked to make sure there was no one in the nearby vicinity, and then headed down a sandy beach trail that took him to his extraction point.

Sixty-five miles away, the Aircraft Carrier USS *Theodore Roosevelt* (CVN 71) and its Battle Group were taking part in UNITAS, the annual U.S./South American Naval Exercise. A UH60 Black Hawk Helicopter launched off of the flight deck of the *Roosevelt*, and began to fly toward Caracas, seemingly undergoing a training exercise. The sleek, black helicopter never flew above 75 feet; the pilot was keen on staying off the radar screen.

As Bastos reached his extraction point, he started signaling his ride home with his flashlight. Once he could see the helo, the pilots with their night vision goggles brought the helicopter into a hover, extracted their package and promptly returned to the *Roosevelt*, undetected.

As he stepped foot on the carrier, Bastos smiled to himself. "*Damn. I'm good.*" He was met at the Carrier's Island (adjacent spot three on the angel deck) by the Battle Group Commander, Rear Admiral Riley Mixon and they were escorted to his quarters by one of the Marine Security guards.

"Agent Miller! Congratulations on a successful op."

"Thank you, sir. You know I'm not one to brag, but I think I did a pretty kick-ass job myself."

"Undoubtedly so. However, don't get too relaxed. There's been an urgent request that you report back in Washington. You're needed for something big back there."

Bastos laughed. "No rest for the wicked, huh, Admiral?"

Riley smiled. "No, I don't believe there is. Especially not for you. Take my Flag Quarters, clean yourself up, because you smell like shit, and then rest up. We'll have a helicopter fly you off the ship to Rosy Roads Naval Base, Puerto Rico tomorrow. From there you'll grab a plane to Washington. Understood?"

"Yes sir. Thank you Admiral."

CHAPTER FIVE

THE BRIEF

The Raven Rock Mountain Complex, also known as "Site R", was the location that was designated by President Fletcher to discuss the urgent matter of Flight IA 0000. Often referred to as the "Underground Pentagon", this site was chosen for the COMPARTMENTED, Top Secret meeting instead of Washington due to the magnitude of the talent that was gathered there. The military complex bustled with activity as the United States' most important military fighters and leaders converged upon Site R.

All of the VIPs had arrived at Andrews Air Force Base via different means, and from there they were shuttled in a VH60N White Hawk to the Helipad at the West Gate at Site R.

As Sweetwater stepped out of the government issued White Hawk, he could feel the sense of urgency in the air. There were no jokes or quips; today was all about business. As he was led into the facility itself, Matt couldn't help but think about the precarious position the United States was in. Any outright military action against Iran would cause a backlash, not only globally but on the home front as well. Two long wars had sapped the American public's interest in tedious, drawn out conflicts. At the same time, to sit back and do nothing would be to allow Iran to become a nuclear power, and the thought of that sent shivers down Matt's spine. Whatever was done, it would have to be quick, precise, and violent.

After being led down a long series of corridors that never seemed to stop, Capt. Matt Sullivan finally reached the war room. As he passed through the threshold, there were many discussions being fielded throughout the room as to what was going to be done to cauterize this festering sore.

The war room itself was dominated by a large oval, oak wood table. At the head of the table was the president's seat, which was a large, black leather chair. Above the chair, a green felt cloth was draped, signifying the seat's importance. The president had not yet arrived, so the seat was empty. To the right of the president's seat was the Honorable Larry Blumberg, the Secretary of Defense. To the left was Admiral Tim Lafleur, the Chief of Naval Operations. The rest of the dignitaries were seated in accordance to their ranks, from the most senior to the juniors. Matt found the seat with the label "Capt. Matt Sullivan, CAG" and sat down.

The United States' most important leaders were all gathered in one room. Sweetwater recognized many, but on the other hand, there were a few that he did not recognize. Sitting across the table from him was CIA Agent Craig "Bastos" Miller, Commander Tommy "Pig" Bowman, Gunnery Sergeant Buck "Savage" Cassidy, and Major Chris "Herc" Valentine USAF, MQ9 Reaper

Controller. Seated directly beside him was Capt. Dale "Slick" Morley, Commanding Officer of the *USS Ronald Reagan* (CVN-76) and up the table from him was Vice Admiral Mark Balmert, Commander of the Third Fleet.

It was difficult to understand what anyone was saying, as they were all talking at once. The chatter seemed to reach a maximum before the large oak doors opened. Once the doors opened Capt. Jacobson barked, "All rise!" Instantly, silence filled the room and everyone came to attention and stood up. President Fletcher, Admiral LaFleur and The Honorable Larry Blumberg escorted the president to the table and then took their respective seats. Despite her small stature, she immediately commanded the utmost respect and undying loyalty of everyone in the room.

"Thank you so much for patiently waiting, gentleman," she said in a soft, but strong voice. "Today decisions will be made that are going to change the world; we are going to plan events that will be written down in the history books. Therefore, I ask each of you to think deeply upon what you say—the fate of the free world depends on it." With that, the president motioned for everyone to be seated.

"Secretary Blumberg, would you care to fill us in?" Irene asked. Bloomberg nodded, stood up, and cleared his throat.

"As all of you are undoubtedly aware, Iran has just powered up the Russian-built Nuclear Power Plant in Bushehr. We've known for a long time that Iran has had nuclear ambitions, but that's all they were, mere ambitions. This is the first major step that they've taken towards realizing that goal. I'm sure I don't need to tell you that a nuclear-armed Iran is terrifying. The amount of power that they could project throughout the Middle East would singlehandedly dash any hopes of peace that we've spent years trying to achieve."

Before he continued, the Secretary of Defense put a map on the projector in the room. The map was of the entire world, and a bold red line was drawn from Tehran, Iran to Caracas, Venezuela. "That however, is not where the most pressing concern lies. We've been tracking an airplane, which is signified as Flight IA 0000. This airplane originated seemingly out of nowhere, and flies a consistent route from Tehran to Caracas, Venezuela. Its flight path and its timing are like clockwork."

He moved to the next slide, which consisted of several photos of Flight IA 0000. "Normally, we'd think nothing of it, but this plane originated the week before the Bushehr Power Plant came back online. The plane seemed to carry no passengers, and is parked in two newly built hangars in Caracas and Tehran. Other than that, we knew nothing about it. That is, until we sent Agent Craig Miller to Caracas to bring us updated information. Agent Miller, would you please enlighten the group?"

"Yes Sir, Mr. Secretary." Larry Blumberg took his seat, and Agent Miller stood up.

"For the last several weeks, I've been on a covert op in Caracas trying to figure out anything I could on Flight IA 0000. As you can see here"—Craig moved to the next slide, which showed satellite photographs of trucks coming and going from the hangars in Tehran and Caracas, along with the photos he'd taken while inside the plane in Caracas—"The Iranians are moving enriched uranium from Tehran to Caracas. Trucks from the Bushehr Nuclear Plant are transporting this enriched uranium to Tehran and flown on Flight IA 0000 to the Simon Bolivar International Airport in Maiquetia, Venezuela, about 13 miles (21kilometers) from downtown Caracas. From the Airport, they're trucking the uranium to several locations, where they're building weapons of mass destruction."

At this point General Sealock, The Director of NSA, stood up.

"NSA has worked tirelessly trying to find out who, if anyone, was the mastermind behind Iran's new obsession with Nuclear Power. What we found"—he flipped to the next slide—"was this man: Tayyib Al'Qim. He is the Middle East's foremost expert on Nuclear Physics, and an avid opponent of the United States. He's written several essays and excerpts on the need for the Middle East to rise up like a nuclear phoenix and challenge the West, but nobody has ever seemed to listen to him. Nobody, until now."

"Conveniently, he's been working at the University of Bushehr, just several miles away from the Power Plant itself. He's been witnessed going to and from the power plant, many, many times. Whatever is happening in Iran, this is the man in charge."

Once "Black Jack" had finished, the room was silent. The most powerful people in the world just simply stared at each other, unable and unsure of what to say. What could they say? The end of the world was at their doorstep, and nobody was ready to answer the door.

Finally, Irene Fletcher spoke up, in a soft voice. "As

you can see gentlemen, this is no joke. What we are dealing with here threatens not only our way of life, but humanity's way of life. We simply cannot let Iran have their way with this." She then paused, making sure to look at everyone in the room. "The question is, what do we do about it?"

After a few seconds of silence, a flurry of ideas, ranging from diplomacy to an outright invasion of Iran, began echoing through the closed doors of the compartmented briefing. The next forty-five minutes was a series of rebuttals, arguments, and faulty schemes. Nothing was panning out, and everyone in the room was growing tired of disagreeing.

Admiral LaFleur, who had until this point been relatively silent, spoke up. "Whatever we have to do, it has to be done quickly. This has to be a get-in, get-out situation. We can't get stuck in another ground war, and the months it would take for a diplomatic solution to take place is exactly what Iran wants. They'd have a full-fledged nuclear program by the time anyone agreed to anything." Everyone in the war room nodded their heads in agreement.

"What we need is a good, old-fashioned one-two punch. If we take out the power plant and Mr. Tayyib Al'Qim, Iran will have no choice but to stop what they're doing. Think about it—we have the world's most powerful air force in the world, and sitting in this room is one of the greatest snipers on record! Why don't we use them? We bomb the power plant, and we have Gunny send Al'Qim six feet under."

President Fletcher stared intently at the Admiral, seeming to search into his soul. For LaFleur, it seemed like an eternity passed before she said, "I like it. It's quick, powerful, and it will show the world that we mean business. Does anyone disagree with the CNO's plan?"

No one disagreed.

"Then it's settled. Admiral LaFleur, prep the Navy for an airstrike on the power plant itself, Gunnery Sergeant Cassidy, prepare yourself for the shot of our life. And as for you, Agent Miller, strap on your fedora and bullwhip— we're going to set you up as a new physics professor at the University of Bushehr.

At this point President Fletcher stood, and everyone came to attention.

"Don't get too excited, gentleman. We aren't done here yet. I need all of you to break down into groups and figure out the exact plan of the assault. I want the complete game plan on my desk within a week. This operation will from now on be known as 'Rolling Thunder'.

As she turned to leave, she said, "It's time for the 'Big Dog to Bark'. Godspeed, gentleman. With that, she and The Secretary of Defense departed.

CHAPTER SIX

CARRIER WORK-UPS

The officers and government agents who attended the brief at Raven Rock returned to their respective commands and agencies. The military officers who were at the meeting from Carrier Strike Force Foxtrot were about to start their work-ups in preparation for their upcoming seven month deployment.

Prior to getting underway for their first three weeks at sea, Capt. Sullivan spent two days in pre-sail conferences with his Air Wing Commanding Officers and their respective department heads. He was in a constant flurry of meetings, planning out attacks, stratagems, and exercises in preparation for operation "Rolling Thunder". It only took a few days—though to him, it felt like two weeks—but they had finally turned "Rolling Thunder" from an idea to a reality.

The plan itself was almost deceptively simple a simultaneous strike on both the Bushehr Power Plant via an airstrike and Tayyib Al'Qim via a bullet, courtesy of Gunny Buck "Savage" Cassidy. A few hours before that, Major Herc Valentine and his crew would use an MQ-9

Reaper drone to shoot down Flight IA 0000. That's where the simplicity ended—to coordinate such a precise strike required a well-tuned war machine. Sweetwater would lead the strike with several other appointed pilots from the airwing. His job over the upcoming pre-deployment months was to put the strike package together that would quickly and expertly deliver a payload in the middle of hostile enemy airspace. Before they shipped out that Monday, the airwing and battle group members took the weekend off, so Matt spent the weekend looking for a place to house Boomer while at sea and to say *yet another goodbye* to Mary Farrio.

As he approached the driveway to his house in La Jolla, Boomer began to bark excitedly and ran in front of his four-runner. Matt's neighbors had been caring for his dog while he was in Washington and for the several days while he was engaged in the pre-sail meetings.

"I know buddy, I know. I'm finally back home," Sweetwater said, as he put the four-runner into park and started to get out. His German Shorthaired Pointer almost knocked him back into his seat with excitement. Boomer barreled into the backyard and started rolling in the freshly cut grass while Sweetwater unloaded the SUV. "Don't get too comfortable buddy! We're gonna have to leave soon!" Matt called out to the dog, but Boomer kept on rolling."

Chuckling to himself, Sweetwater set to work on getting ready for his three weeks at sea. After unloading some groceries and starting his laundry, he called Mary Farrio.

"Hello?" she answered.

"Mary! This is Matt Sullivan."

"Oh Matt! I was hoping you'd call. How was your trip to Washington? Have you saved the world yet?"

Matt laughed. "Nah, not yet! Give me some time. I thought you might like to join me for dinner tonight. I'm leaving Monday for several weeks at sea, and as you can imagine, my schedule is going to start to get pretty busy until we deploy."

"Sure, I'd love to! Anything I need to bring?"

"Nope! Just yourself, sweetheart. How does seven o'clock sound?"

"Seven, got it. See you then!"

Mary arrived right at seven. Matt poured her some wine, and they sat in his backyard overlooking the ocean. Boomer was still racing and rolling around.

Matt barbecued steaks while the potatoes and corn cooked. After dinner they watched the sunset and talked about the weeks past.

When the timing was right, Matt paused, collecting his thoughts, before he continued.

"I know this is crazy, because we've only known each other for a short time but . . . I'm crazy about you. I hadn't planned on meeting an amazing woman only to be gone most of the time so early in the relationship."

"Matt, I—"

"I know this is probably an awful thing to ask but . . . can you wait for me? After our work-ups, I'll then be deployed overseas until February. Maybe you could meet me in Singapore during our mid-cruise port call?"

"Singapore? Hmmm. Any idea on when that would be?"

Although Matt knew the exact date, because it

was classified he couldn't divulge it, simply replied, "mid-November."

"You know what, yes. That sounds exciting; I've never been to Singapore!"

Matt smiled, and leaned in to kiss her. "If things work out, I'll send you a ticket along with our in-port information and if you can get away, I'd love to see you. It would surely break up the long deployment."

Mary reached over and kissed Matt. He kissed her back. It led to a passionate weekend.

As it was getting close to noon on Sunday, Matt yelled to Boomer, "Come on, boy!" He put Boomers' toys in the back seat and yelled again, "Buddy, we gotta go!"

Boomer rounded the corner and hopped in the backseat.

"Alright buddy," Matt said as he got in the truck and turned the ignition. "Found you a place that you're gonna stay while I'm away."

Boomer looked up at Matt, perplexed.

"I know buddy. I'm not a fan of leaving you either."

Matt drove to a ranch just outside of San Diego.

"Alright Boomer, here we are." Boomer whimpered. He knew something was wrong. "Hey buddy, I know. This sucks, but it's gotta happen. I can't take you with me. You know how much shit you'd cause on an Aircraft Carrier?" he said as he scratched Boomer behind the ears. "So, I found you a place! Remember the Flintoms? You haven't seen them since you were a puppy, but they love you!"

Matt opened up the car door and walked out with Boomer.

"I mean, look at this place, buddy! Wide open spaces,

other dogs to play with, horses to chase and terrorize." He looked at Boomer, who looked back up at him. "This is paradise, isn't it?"

"Matt Sullivan!" A man yelled from the house. "Glad to see you made it!"

"Dr. Flintom! Absolutely! How are you?"

"Doin' quite well, son. And look who we have here? Boomer! You're all grown up!" Boomer barked.

"Seriously, thank you so much for doing this. Didn't have much time to plan; you know how these things go. He's a good boy, though. Right Boomer?" The dog looked up at him inquisitively.

"Oh I'm sure he is. And don't worry about it. You just stay safe out there, you hear?"

"Roger that." Matt knelt down to pet Boomer. "Alright buddy, you be a good boy, okay? I mean it." Boomer started to whimper. "It's alright, Boom. I'm gonna be back in a few weeks. Deal?" Boomer whimpered again. "I know, buddy. Take care of yourself." He gave Boomer one more scratch and stood up.

"Once again doc, thank you so much. I'll be back to pick him up in three weeks," Matt said as he turned to walk back toward his four-runner.

"Don't worry, Boomer will be well cared for. We'll be here until you get back!"

Matt headed back to his home in La Jolla, packed his sea-bag and locked up his home. Sweetwater always liked to board the ship the night before it got underway, to avoid traffic jams and the threat of "missing movement", (the ship leaving port, without him) the day the ship sailed.

Once the *USS Ronald Reagan* (CVN-76) cleared the breakwater past Point Loma and headed for the open sea, general quarters (GQ) was sounded throughout the ship. The squadron personnel are only aboard when the air-wing is onboard, and ship's company who are attached to the *USS Reagan* are always aboard the ship until their tour is up with that particular ship. However, the air wing personnel had been cleaning their assigned spaces and living quarters for over a month, making ready for when the ship sets sail for their work-ups and deployment. Therefore, they knew their assigned GQ stations.

Preparing a crew for GQ is just as important as carrying out "Rolling Thunder" and is tantamount to carrying it out successfully. GQ cannot be left to the imagination that anyone will know what to do, where to go, what not to do or where not to go upon hearing the klaxon sound for GQ, nor is there such a thing as "too much" preparedness. The very nature of any emergency dictates that it can happen, any place and with anyone present or in charge. As such, numerous drills are a normal part of a crew's life, and often become monotonous, but still necessary. Timing for having the ship "at" GQ is essential from the moment it's sounded until the captain is informed that the ship is secure. If one crewmember is unaccounted for at the assigned battle station, that department head cannot yet report 'all hands present and accounted for' thereby rendering the entire ship 'not at' GQ. During a drill, a certain time period is pre-arranged wherein missing personnel are considered officially unaccounted for, and the department head reports readiness with X number of persons missing, reason unknown. Training drills must be run at various times of the day and night and introduce various scenarios that mirror potential threats.

Engine men, hull technicians, boiler technicians, and nuclear reactor units must report to their work space. Command center, combat center, bridge, and communications personnel must report to their assigned locations as well. Crew members assigned to shipboard aviation units or duties report to either the flight deck, hangar deck, fueling stations. Pilots and flight crew report to their ready rooms and be ready to launch if necessary. Medical personnel report to sick-bay, or triage spaces. Damage control teams report to either their workspaces or points of vulnerability throughout the ship. In all cases, real or drills, everyone on the ship has an assigned place to go and a job to fulfill.

After general quarters, Capt. Matt Sullivan, Air Wing Eleven Commander, welcomed his air wing officers and enlisted personnel aboard. The collective manpower totaled close to three thousand.

Later in the day, Capt. Morley, the *Reagan's* commanding officer, made this statement over the 1MC (a shipboard public address circuit on U.S. Navy Vessels). "Today is the beginning of 'Carrier Work-ups', these next three weeks are going to be grueling with drills, flight operations and general quarters, twice a day. The first aircraft will not start to come aboard for another week. This will allow you to become familiar with the ship and its operations. If this is your first work-up period aboard the *Reagan*, know your job, stay hydrated and maintain situational awareness at all times. Watch out for your shipmates and let's have a safe and productive three weeks. That's all, captain out."

After three vigorous weeks at sea, Air Wing Eleven was carrier qualified and all drills were performed satisfactorily. Prior to pulling into port, Capt. Morley, the *Reagan's* (CVN-76) Commanding Officer, CAG Sullivan, Airwing Eleven's Commander and Rear Admiral Coleman, the Carrier Strike Force Foxtrot Commander all had a meeting with Cmdr. Mike "Bearskin" Beresky, the *Reagan's* Air Boss. Everyone commented on how well the F-35C *Lightning* aircraft performed and integrated with the rest of the air wing. Capt. Nick "Ralphy Boy" Petriccione, the Commanding Officer of VFA 105 Gunslingers, personally received a well done from all, stating what a tremendous job he'd done preparing his squadron to go to sea for the first time with the new F-35C aircraft.

Rear Admiral Coleman spoke, "The Lightning's maneuverability on the flight deck and hangar deck has been well-received by the handling crew. They all say it is by far one of the best aircraft they've ever dealt with. And on top of that, its boarding rate was phenomenal compared to the rest of the airwing. All in all, these bad boys are fitting in perfectly with the carrier environment."

Carrier Strike Group Eleven had two weeks in port before they went back to sea. Sweetwater headed up to the Flintom's ranch to pick-up Boomer. They enjoyed his company and said he was a perfect guest, which made Matt feel at ease. A day before the carrier went to sea for the second time Matt dropped Boomer off again and returned to his home in La Jolla. This time, he'd be flying out to the ship from NAS North Island. Sweetwater had a 0900 overhead, which meant, once the carrier was off the coast, heading towards Whiskey 291 Operating Area, he would lead a flight of four F-35's out to the ship, circle overhead until they got a Signal Charlie from the Air Boss, clearing them to come into the break and land. Matt had left most of his military clothing on the carrier from the trip before, along with other items he would need while at sea. Therefore, he packed a small duffel-bag of items he needed, which fit into a storage compartment on his plane.

The night before Sullivan headed out to sea, many of the junior officers gathered at a local watering hole in Coronado called, "The Outhouse." Lt. Gary "BigHands" Johnson and other pilots from the airwing, who were walking aboard, were at the bar throwing back a few beers. The JOs (junior officers) were singing war songs at the top of their lungs, and just being generally boisterous, when this bombshell of a woman walked in the bar. Within a second, all eyes were on her.

She was a tall drink of water, 5'9", with short, blonde hair. She was wearing a tight, leather jacket that read "Harley Motorcycles" on the back. She walked sultrily to the bar and ordered Jack on the Rocks. She was hot, and she knew it. So did everybody else.

As Chad prepared her drink, the group of loud aviators were using their hands as planes and discussing how they were shooting down bogie's (enemy aircraft) with their fighter planes. Once they saw her though, their conversation changed.

"Damn. Look at that. Mmmmhmmm."

"Absolutely. Wouldn't mind having myself a taste of that."

"Shut up, Dirt. You're all talk."

"I'm all talk? If I was all talk, I wouldn't do this," Dirt said as he gulped down the last of his beer, and approached the busty blonde.

"Hey missy," he said.

The woman rolled her eyes. "Can I help you?"

"Man, you're hot. So hot, I know it, you know it, and everybody else in here knows it. I just want to get to know you a little better. What's your name, girl?"

The woman smiled. "Really? Just want to get to know me? No other intentions?"

"Just want to know your name. That's all. Scouts honor," Dirt slurred.

"Nicky. Nicky Mather. You can call me 'Siren' though."

"Ohhhh Siren? I like that. So what's a girl like you doing in a place like this?"

Nicky laughed. "I'm with CAG Eleven Air Wing, I'm a helicopter pilot."

"No shit? A helicopter pilot? Wouldn't have guessed you were in the military."

"Well, you know what they say: don't judge a book by its cover."

"Well, you're right about that." Dirt leaned in closer. "So, where did you go to school?"

"The Naval Academy. Listen, I'm flattered by your interest in me, but I'm just waiting for some friends, and I'd like to just have a drink to relax."

Dirt got bold, and moved his hand right up on her ass. "Listen baby, I just want to relax too. Why don't we relax toge—" He was cut off by the sound of his own head smashing down on the hard wooden bar. He fell down to the floor, out cold.

Nicky sighed. The bartender looked at her.

"I know, I know. I'm leaving. Thanks for the drink," she said, as she paid and left a generous tip.

With that, she walked out the front door, hopped on her motorcycle, and drove off.

This at-sea period was going to be much more intense with long days and nights. The air wing would be simulating air strikes on specific targets and there would be a lot of ordnance dropped. There were to be four single-cycle launches lasting between one and two hours and three double cycle launches lasting three plus hours. Each launch had a minimum of seven aircraft pre-launches, with a max of twelve. Air Wing Eleven's flight deck ordnance crew and the USS Reagan's ordnance crew had worked very closely together during this line period. They needed to ensure correct bombs and bullets were on the flight deck in a timely fashion, so the air wing's ordnance crews could load the planes for the next turn-around launch.

The ship's flight deck handling crew would be training new personnel and getting their skills back up to speed. And although the deck of the carrier is a stationary, bland steel hue, during a launch it becomes a colorful experience full of non-stop movement; the Yellow Shirts (who taxi the aircraft on the flight deck), the Purple Shirts (who refuel the planes), the Brown Shirts (who are the air wing's plane captains who assist the pilots during man-ups), the Blue Shirts (who chock and chain the aircraft to the flight deck), the Green Shirts (who work the catapult and arresting gear), the Red Shirts (who attach and remove the ordnance), the White Shirts (who ensure safety), and the Red Shirts in firefighting suits (who standby in case of a crash). During a large launch, there can be anywhere from two to three hundred people running around the flight deck. This is why everyone has to keep their heads on a swivel and watch out for their buddies. Otherwise, personnel can get sucked down engine intakes, cut in half by propeller blades, blown overboard or get run over. These are just a few of the hazards of working on the flight deck of an aircraft carrier. It is paramount that the ship's personnel and air wing crew work as a cohesive unit during flight operations.

CHAPTER SEVEN
CIRCLE THE WAGONS

It was close to 1300, and the airwing pilots had refreshed their carrier landings. All eighty-two aircraft were back on board for their next at-sea period. CAG Sullivan completed his traps (arrested landings) relatively early on and was observing the rest of his pilots while they finished up.

What he didn't know was Boomer's growing restlessness, "at the dog sitter's house".

Matt had been gone for two days and wasn't aware of how anxious Boomer had become. The Flintom's noticed he hadn't eaten much since he arrived, but they felt it was normal until Boomer settled in for his next visit. However, Boomer's anxiety was much worse than they realized. He spent most of the first day, and half the night, looking at the front driveway, waiting for his bud to come back and pick him up. Boomer may have been just a dog, but his canine instinct was telling him, something wasn't right. And just like his master, he wasn't going to let it happen lying down.

Boomer waited until night had fallen on his second day when things at the ranch were quiet. The humans were sleeping peacefully, and the other animals were nowhere to be found. The Flintom's had Boomer in a nice enclosure in their back yard. There was a big area to run and a small tack barn Boomer had access to if he needed to get out of the weather. The small wooden fence that surrounded the back yard kept Boomer in by choice, but he wasn't about to be caged in any longer. Early morning on the third day, Boomer decided it was time to "cut and run." While gaining speed, he leaped over the fence and headed out across the pasture and down the road where he saw Matt depart, hoping to find him around the next bend in the road.

The third day at sea was a big one; there were seven launches scheduled, which would last until the wee hours of the following morning. Lt. Commander Nicky Mather (Siren) was on the first launch as plane guard. Her MH-60R Helicopter was equipped with full SAR (search and rescue) gear. She would ensure all aircraft were safely airborne after the first launch and then safely recovered back aboard the carrier.

Before Siren launched, she was getting breakfast in Wardroom Two, better known as the "Dirty Shirt Locker." It got its nickname, because pilots and flight deck crews could eat their meals in flight suits and work clothes. In Wardroom One, you had to be in the uniform of the day. Only officers could eat in Wardrooms One and Two. The enlisted crew had many galleys they could gather at for their meals, where the uniform of the day was not required.

While Nicky was getting her toast, she noticed Lt. John (Dirt) Day, from VFA-22, "The Fighting Redcocks" Squadron that was in her air wing. He was the gent she'd drop-checked in the bar, several days prior.

As he walked past her, she said, "Hey Lieutenant, that's a big knot you have on your lid."

When Dirt realized who she was, he said out loud, "Well I'll be goddamned, if it isn't Siren. Holy shit gal, you pack a hell of a wallop."

"That's probably because I have a second degree black-belt in Taekwondo and you were four sheets to the wind."

Dirt laughed. "Well, do you mind if I join you?"

Siren laughed, "Heck no, come over and have a seat." The two sat and had breakfast together and mended any hardships they may have fostered.

As they were leaving, Capt. Sullivan took a seat across from them.

"Morning CAG," they both enthusiastically bellowed.

"Morning," he replied. "Great day to go flying, wouldn't you say?"

"Yes sir, sure is," they replied, as they headed over to the counter to dump their trays. While CAG was pouring syrup on his French toast, a sickening feeling passed through his gut. Thinking it was just light gas, he didn't pay much attention to it. For some reason, at that moment of uneasiness, he thought of Boomer.

Day turned into night, and night turned into morning, and another day passed as Boomer continued on his long journey to find his soul mate. His pace had lessened, but not too much. His powerful legs were still churning out lengthy strides, his tongue sticking out of his mouth, panting. His run turned into a walk after crossing a small ridge, before he reached a highway. Boomer stopped to rest by a clump of trees, at the crest of the hill. He could see the early morning sunrise over a multitude of lights near the ocean; he was sure his master was somewhere close.

Boomer gingerly walked down the hill to the edge of the highway. It was a four-lane speed fest, running north and south, with a division of grass keeping the two sections from meeting. The dog waited his turn as several cars zoomed past him. He saw an opening after a large semi had passed, and he took it. He lunged forward, clearing the highway in a few short bounds.

As his paws patted the green earth below, he readied himself to cross the next section of highway. Cars were flying past, with no respite in sight. Boomer began to grow impatient, testing himself to see if he had the courage to cross the dangerous highway without a gap. Finally, he saw his chance in between a large white truck and a green SUV so he took it. He leaped directly behind the white truck, crouched in, and jumped forward again, barely missing the green SUV. He landed on green grass, and tumbled down the slope of a hill.

Boomer stopped to catch his breath. Between him and the glow of lights was a small forest. He was exhausted, "going days" without food or sufficient water intake was beginning to take a toll on him. He found a small bog of brackish water and took several sips before he curled up next to a fallen tree and rested.

After breakfast, CAG went to VFA-86's an F/A-18's ready room, (the Sidewinders). He briefed his four plane flight, which would be dropping thirty or so "Blue Blaster Bombs" (25 lbs. bombs) on R2510, the site named for the Loom Lobby Target Range near El Centro. Lt.

Commander Brown, the "Big Bopper", Lt. Day and two other Squadron-Mates, would be hitting targets on the Chocolate Mountain Aerial Gunnery Range (CMGAR). The eight plane launch was scheduled for an 0800 go.

Lt. Cmdr. Mather manned up her bird at 0730 on spot three, which was on the angle deck, just forward of catapults three and four. Once rotors were turning and all systems were a go, she lifted off the flight deck at 0745 and assumed a racetrack pattern, 500 feet on the starboard side of the Carrier's Island; awaiting the first fixed-wing launch of the day at 0800.

After his rest, Boomer stepped over the remains of a dead tree. As he cleared it, he heard the snap of twigs behind him. The hairs on his back began to rise indicating danger. He quickly looked behind him, and saw nothing. To his left was a rustle in the brush and he saw something move, but wasn't sure of its nature. Boomer barked, and began to growl, challenging whatever was tormenting him to come out.

As he stood still, he began to see objects circling around him like a group of Conestoga wagon's readying for the evening's events. His growling and barking became louder and louder as he began to look to his left and right. From behind a large fir tree in front of him, he heard a howl; then behind him, he heard another noise. Boomer stopped, and looked directly at where the first sound came from. Out from behind the tree stalked a large coyote, with piercing yellow eyes, and then behind him, a smaller coyote appeared. The coyote directly in front of him had a scar above its right eye, which it seemed to wear with pride, like a war wound. The coyote stood still and snapped its teeth at Boomer, then began to growl profusely. Boomer quickly turned and charged the smaller animal behind him, which made him retreat. Then he quickly snapped around and bared his teeth as well at the larger coyote. Lowering his front legs, preparing himself for a charge, the coyote leapt forward, teeth bared. Boomer jumped to the side, missing the coyote's teeth by the fraction of an inch. The coyote snapped, angry that it had missed its prey. Boomer didn't rest on his laurels; he jumped right back and sunk his teeth into the coyote's neck. The second coyote started to approach, but stopped for some reason and backed down.

The coyote in distress howled, shook its neck vigorously, causing Boomer to fly off, smashing into a nearby oak tree. The coyote lunged at Boomer, who was still trying to collect himself. Boomer felt the coyote's teeth sink into his back, tearing through fur and flesh. The German Shorthaired Pointer let out a yelp, and struggled to release himself from the vice-grip of the coyote's teeth. As he struggled, the coyote growled, almost contentedly, as if he knew that he had won.

Boomer wasn't ready to give up the ghost; he used his hind legs to hurl the coyote off of his back. As Boomer straightened himself out, he could feel the blood running down his coat. His instinctual behavior became his strategy. The first coyote was bigger, and stronger, plus he didn't know where the other coyote was hiding. He wouldn't win a fair fight, if the two coyotes teamed up on him, so he had to react fast. The bigger coyote was in front of a dead tree, which was lying on its side on the ground.

The coyote howled, begging Boomer to come for him.

Boomer readied himself, and then charged—but he didn't charge the coyote himself. Instead, he gathered momentum and leapt onto the dead tree, gaining a height advantage. As the coyote turned around to face this new threat, Boomer jumped, teeth bared, right onto the coyote's back. Boomer sunk his teeth into the coyote's neck, and then held on for dear life. The coyote thrashed around, but Boomer refused to let go. Finally, the coyote's fits of rage became the last cries of a dying animal, and then it lay still. Boomer had won and the smaller of the two coyotes was nowhere in sight.

Boomer released his grip on the coyote, and shambled past its body and the large oak tree. He managed to pass through the small forest itself, and was able to view a group of homes upon the city by the bay. He tried to take a step forward, but collapsed. The lack of food and water, along with the loss of blood had taken its toll. Boomer whimpered, and struggled to get back on his feet, but he couldn't. Every attempt caused him to fall. Finally, it became too much for him, and even though he tried to fight it, Boomer crawled with his front paws under a mossy log and closed his eyes.

CHAPTER EIGHT

THE SHED

The Commanding Officer of SEAL Team Six chose his Red Squadron Commander, Tommy "Pig" Bowman, to lead and train Gunny Buck Cassidy on the covert op to kill Tayyib Al'Qim. He could count on him to keep his mouth shut about the details; he had the SDV (SEAL Delivery Vehicle) background from his previous tour of duty in Hawaii. While there he conducted many sensitive missions that he didn't share with others in his squadron. He did need, however, a break from the Afghanistan rotations where he lost two of his closest friends and the best combat assault dog ever assigned to his unit. Under his command on the new mission to kill was Lieutenant Commander 'Wiz' Anderson from SPECWARCOM, a jack of all trades, supreme SEAL warrior, along with SOC "Hawk" Baker, medic and coxswain and SO3 "Maggot" Malone, the AW (Automatic Weapon) gunner. These SEALs were handpicked because of this high risk, high-payoff mission. Operation "Rolling Thunder" at this end had to be rehearsed and orchestrated in mind numbing detail. Any deviations traditionally meant mission failure and often death for the men out on the pointy end of the spear.

Cmdr. Bowman was a man you would not want to face in a fight. He was 43 years old, 6'2" and chiseled like a champion wrestler. Although his big bushy brown mustache was his trademark, he was all business and scary looking. He and his team would be training Gunnery Sergeant "Buck" Cassidy in the Dry Deck Shelter (DDS), better known as the SHED.

Bowman hadn't seen Buck since the meeting at Raven Rock; however, they would be meeting up this evening at McP's Irish Pub in Coronado. Gunny took several days leave after the briefing to be with his family, who he hadn't seen for eight months, while deployed to Afghanistan.

At 2000 on the dot, Gunny Buck walked into McP's, a SEAL watering hole and the first thing he heard was a loud "HOO YAH" from Pig, sitting at the corner left stool at the end of the bar by the entrance.

"Evening Sir," said Buck. "How you doing?"

"Great, let's have a few beers and I'll take you down to the base and check you into your quarters."

The next several weeks were going to be intensive for Buck, but being a SOCOM Marine readied him for the task. He would get intensive DDS (Dry Deck Shelter) familiarization and dive refresher training with the experts. Wiz had him first for "drown-proofing" and other swim related programs that prepared him for the SHED's lock-in and lock-out procedures. Hawk familiarized him with rubber duck ocean operation, dealing with the surf and losing a man over the side. Maggot, meanwhile, honed his BLR Lightning rifle skills while on the weapons range. The rifle has state of the art accuracy that projects a magnum bullet precisely where it's intended.

The rifle was lightweight and easy to pack. This would be the rifle Buck would use in his attempt to kill Tayyib Al'Qim. However, the most important training came from Cmdr. Bowman, with his familiarization training in the DDS, which would be attached on the back of the *USS Michigan*, an SSGN nuclear submarine. Buck was soon to learn, "The Only Easy Day Was Yesterday".

Wiz, Hawk and Maggot put Buck through his paces. He went from one constant training to another; runs on the beach, swims, boat drills, PT and gunnery shooting, which intentionally created non-stop stress and strain to help reinforce his endurance. Dealing with the "Rubber Duck" in the ocean gave Buck some trouble with over-turning in the surf. After several speed-slaps from Hawk, he finally got the technique and became pretty good at it.

The night before Cassidy was to start his DDS training was a restless one, because he'd never been exposed to anything like this before. Even though he'd been trained as a "Tunnel Rat" and as a sniper, this was going to be a true challenge. Although Buck was a very talented sniper and battle-hardened Marine, he was very apprehensive about the claustrophobic underwater experience of the DDS lock-in/lock-out. Even though he made it through dive school in Key West and he did what he had to do, he was damn glad he wasn't a SEAL on an SDV Team. He much preferred being a sniper on land.

The *USS Michigan* was fitted with a removable module which attached aft of the sub's sail, allowing the SEALs and divers easy exit and entrance while the sub is submerged. The *USS Michigan* was specifically selected to join Carrier Strike Force Foxtrot due to its capability of housing the SHED. The modification to the sub called for an appropriate hatch configuration, electrical connections, piping for ventilation, diver's air and water drainage capability.

A DDS is thirty eight feet long, nine feet high and wide. It can hold eight or nine members; it's dark, cramped, and claustrophobic under the best of circumstances. All members in the SHED have to know and understand how to operate it, in case the officer-in-charge becomes incapacitated. Usually divers or the SEALs will remain in the SHED to supervise the controls and run the process of getting the Zodiac gear and guys in and out of the shelter.

Although Buck was making impressive progress with his training, he still needed another week or so to become very comfortable locking in and out of the DDS.

One of Buck's specialties in Afghanistan was flushing out the Taliban in the mountain tunnels. During one particular mission, Buck set off a trip wire which caused a tunnel to cave in on top of him. He was buried alive for several hours. After near death, he never volunteered for another tunnel op. He never realized how claustrophobic he had become until he started working in the SHED. As a result, his acclamation to the SHED took a little longer than usual, but Savage wasn't about to admit that to the SEALs!

CHAPTER NINE

UNIVERSITY OF BUSHEHR

There was a knock on the CIA Director's door. Director Lyle Bien opened it—it was Bastos.

"Agent Miller, I've been expecting you." He motioned for Craig to come in and sit down. "Would you like some coffee?"

"Yes, I'd love some, thank you."

"Cream? Sugar?"

"No sir, just black, thank you."

As Bien poured the coffee he asked, "So, do you understand your orders?"

"Yes Sir," Bastos replied. "My cover name is 'Mohammed Abdul Mani.' I am the new physics professor at Bushehr University. In preparation, I have brushed up on my physics. My PhD paperwork is in order and I'm locked and loaded, ready to go."

Bien handed Craig his coffee. "Excellent. We've arranged diplomatic immunity for your passage into the country and while you are there, you'll also be assisting the head soccer coach for the University."

Agent Miller took a sip of his coffee and said, "Great, I'll be able to brush up on my corner kicks!"

Ho Chi laughed, as he said, "Just don't strain any-thing." He walked over and sat down at his desk before he continued, "Your person of interest is the key to this covert operation. Do you know who he is?"

"Yes sir. The target is Tayyib Al'Qim, who is currently the head of the Physics Department at the University. This is our guy, the one who's responsible for powering up the Bushehr Nuclear Power Plant."

"Very good. I cannot stress enough how important this mission is, which is exactly why we don't have any extraction plans for you at this time. Understood?"

"Yes sir."

"Do you understand how you'll be transmitting infor-mation back to us?"

"Yes sir. Tayyib Al'Qim is an avid Mahjong player, so I will strike up a friendship using that. General Sealock, Capt. Jacobson and I have set up codes using the Mahjong cards to pass along the sensitive intel required for 'Rolling Thunder.' I'll arrange some sort of weekly game on the second and fourth Thursday of each month. Prior to his arrival, I will have the information laid out on the playing board."

"Perfect, then we'll have the ARGUS satellite pass over-head and record your intelligence. Also, we've arranged for you to reside in a small apartment in the seaport vil-lage of Akhtar, about a mile from where Al'Qim will be living, which should make him easily accessible."

Bien looked at Bastos. "Well, it seems like you're ready. I don't want to sound like a broken record, but I can't stress to you enough how important this operation is. 'Rolling Thunder' hinges upon your success. Be careful out there,

Bastos. Sorry for the quick turnaround, but when the "Big Dog Barks," we must answer the call. Your aircraft will be leaving out of Hangar Five today. Stay strong."

"Yes sir."

"Ah! You must be Mohammed Abdul Mani! Please, please do sit down." Agent Miller approached Tayyib Al'Qim's desk and took a seat. His office was magnificent, looking almost like a royal throne rather than a professor's office. Tayyib himself wasn't as imposing as Bastos was expecting. He was a small man, 5'7", with a long grey beard. He had a scar directly above his right eye.

"How is your first day going? Are you getting acquainted with everything?"

"Very much so. It's a beautiful university. I'm very excited for the opportunity to teach here."

"I have no doubt that you are . . . no doubt indeed. Tell me, Mohammed . . . tell me about yourself. You are from America, no?"

"Yes." From New York, originally. I have no love for my country, if that's what you're asking. Not hate either, just indifference. It is my passion to travel the world, to seek the truth. That is what led me here."

"To seek the truth? What truth are you trying to seek?"

"The ultimate truth to the ultimate question: why are we here? I believe I have found that answer in Islam. I converted several years ago, changing my western name to an acceptable Muslim name. As for traveling the world, I've taught physics in several different countries."

"Yes, yes, I see that. Very impressive resume you have here, I must say. Impressive indeed." Tayyib looked at Agent Miller intently. Finally, he said, "I must say, I'm very excited to watch your progress here. I'm sure you'll find this university enlightening. Do you have any questions for me?"

Bastos looked at Tayyib Al'Qim. "Yes, I do. Do you play Mahjong?"

.

CHAPTER TEN

SAND BLOWER FLIGHT

Capt. Sullivan was driving to NAS North Island from his home in La Jolla. He would be flying the F-35C to the ship, which was already at sea. This was the last of five at-sea periods before Carrier Strike Force Foxtrot left on their seven month deployment. As the Air Wing Commander (CAG), Sweetwater was the only pilot qualified to fly the F/A-18 and F-35C on and off the ship for tactical and operational missions.

As he drove over the Coronado Bridge, Matt could only wonder what had happened to Boomer. The Flintoms were noticeably upset as well, due to his disappearance while under their watch. For the last several months both Matt and the veterinarians posted numerous notices in and around the county for Boomerang's safe return, but they had not received any follow-up responses to date.

With the Carrier Strike Force Foxtrot (CSF) one month away from their seven month deployment, Vice Adm. Balmert (3rd Fleet) and his staff, set up a battle scenario for CSF Foxtrot to carry out. The plan was designed to see how well they could defend the Carrier Strike Force Foxtrot and drop bombs on selected targets.

This was a major exercise that lasted four days. If the carrier strike group did not perform in a satisfactory manner, Commanding Officers, Department Heads and key personnel were relieved from their positions. New people would then be assigned their jobs and the drills would be redone until a satisfactory outcome was achieved. Once CENTEX (Certification Exercise Operation) was satisfactorily completed, the carrier strike group would be cleared for deployment.

During the final days of this training exercise, numerous simulated attacks were flown against Carrier Strike Group Eleven, trying to disrupt their effectiveness and destroy their assigned mission targets. The Sand Blower Flight was one of the last events of this exercise, code named, "Enduring Freedom." The flight would be flown at 300 to 500 hundred feet AGL (above ground level) off the deck the entire mission, hitting pre-selected checkpoints along the Sand Blower route.

"Alright gentleman," Matt said to the group, we've spent the last three days surviving air attacks. We've won aerial dogfights, out smarted attacking surface vessels on our escort ships and now, 3rd Fleet is going to see if we can drop bombs and shoot bullets on targets without being detected prior to delivery. That's why our stealth F-35C *Lightning* Squadron has been selected for this Sand Blower mission. As you all know, the Electro-Optical-Distribution Aperture System (DAS) on this aircraft will allow us to get to our selected targets undetected, drop our ordnance and get out of there before anyone is the wiser. This mission was selected for a very specific reason and *it will become more apparent once we're on deployment.* Is that understood?" Sweetwater's speech was greeted with a unanimous, "Yes sir!"

CAG turned on the projector which showed a map of the Sand Blower route. A red line snaked its way through the Santa Barbara mountain range, up through the Northeast side of the Tehachapi Mountains, down to the "Badwater Basin" and into the Amargosa Valley. A giant red "X" was plastered on "Jack Ass Flats"; all pilots had kneeboard cards that resembled the route along with checkpoints marked.

"Once we're off the catapults, we'll all join up at 500ft," CAG reiterated. "Bopper, you'll be in the slot until we go feet dry (sea to land); then climb up to fifteen thousand feet and follow the flight."

"Roger that," replied Bopper.

"Skipper (a name referring to the commanding officer of a squadron) and 'BigHands', once we hit the beach, we'll drop down to four hundred feet and accelerate to 350 knots."

A double ROGER was heard, meaning they both understood.

"We'll go feet dry at Pt. Conception, just north of Santa Barbara. We'll drop down to four hundred feet, go up and over the Santa Barbara Mountain range and fly on the northwest side of the Tehachapi Mountain Range. At Miracle Hot Springs we'll go up and over the Tehachapi range and down into the "Badwater Basin", the lowest point in North America. "I bet you didn't know that "BigHands," CAG said.

"No sir, I did not. Consider me enlightened," replied "BigHands," still green from the F-35C RAG, VFA-101.

CAG laughed, but then went right back to business. "We'll then head to Amargosa Valley, where our targets of interest will be, specifically at "Jack Ass Flats." There will be buses, trucks and tanks as targets. I'll be carrying two AGM-88 HARM Smart Weapons. Skipper Petriccione and BigHands, you'll each have two MK-82 Snake Eye bombs and two MK-20 Rock Eye bombs. As you know from training, our new helmet-mounted display system is deadly accurate and we should be able to level every-thing in sight. Remember, we're making only one run on the targets; make it count. After weapons deployment, we'll pitch-up to fifteen thousand feet turning to a head-ing of two seven zero degrees. At that time, I'll switch the 'Gunslinger Flight' over to the Nellis Missile Range Controller for a Vector to the tanker. "Bopper" will be in a left hand racetrack pattern at fifteen thousand feet over the Tehachapi Mountain range. We'll use Naval Air Station Lemoore as our emergency divert field."

"Okay gents, one last time. I'll be leading the 'Gunslinger Flight' tonight. The flight will consist of three F-35's and one F/A-18. Skipper, you'll be on my left wing, 'BigHands', you'll be on my right wing and 'Bopper' you'll be in the slot flying the F/A-18 tanker aircraft. Any questions?"

"No sir," they replied.

"Okay then, we'll see you on the flight deck."

After evening chow and before the flight crews had to man-up, CAG headed back to his office to finish up some paper work. Bopper went to the hangar deck to check on an engine change his men were working on. Skipper Petriccione went to his office to send a message. BigHands relaxed in the Gunslinger ready room.

At 1815 the pilots headed to their gear lockers and suited up for their 1900 launch. The carrier was steaming towards the northern section of the southern California offshore complex known as SOCAL, named W-291 (whiskey-291). This area is located in the waters adjacent to the southern California coast from Santa Barbara to Baja California.

Fifteen minutes prior to the launch, all aircraft were "turning and burning." The aircraft were located in the Fly Three area of the flight deck, which is in and around the fantail. The Yellow Shirt flight director, standing in front of CAG's F-35C aircraft, gave him a thumbs-up signal, which was asking him, *"Are you ready to taxi?"* When he received a thumbs-up back from the cockpit, he held his fists up at eye level, signaling the pilot to hold his brakes. Then the Yellow-Shirt lowered his hands below his waist and gave a thumb's out to the Blue-Shirt under the aircraft. He was telling him to pull the hard rubber chocks from the tires. Once the chocks had been removed, the Yellow-Shirt moved twenty feet out in front of the aircraft, left or right depending on available space, brought his hands up to eye level, flashed his fingers at the pilot, telling him to release the brakes. At that time, the Yellow Shirt director motioned the pilot to taxi his aircraft. Once the aircraft was close to the Yellow-Shirt directing him, he threw his arms out in front of his chest, passing the taxiing aircraft off to another Yellow-Shirt farther down the flight deck. The same procedure would be done with the other aircraft and they would taxi up the flight deck in trail.

CAG was directed to catapult one; Lt. Johnson went

to catapult two, and therefore, he'd be pulled second from his spot. Once CAG and BigHands had taxied past the Island, (the carrier super structure) "Bopper" was pulled next, because he was going to catapult four, which took some maneuvering to get lined up on the zipper-track for launch. Skipper Petriccione was directed to catapult three.

As CAG was taxiing to line-up on catapult one, a Green-Shirt (catapult personnel) held a weight board up in the air, indicating the weight of the aircraft, which was sixty-five thousand pounds. If the CAG agreed, he would give a thumbs up, if he wanted it lowered, he'd give a cut wave sign in front of his helmet, telling the Green-Shirt to lower the weight. All changes in weights were plus or minus 1000 lbs. Once the aircraft weight had been set, he'd give a thumbs-up, while still taxing for line-up. As he approached for line-up, the Yellow Shirt slowed the aircraft down to a crawl, then put his left arm under his right elbow and dropped his right arm down, telling the pilot to lower his launch bar. CAG continued taxiing with the launch bar down; he taxied up and over the shuttle, a two foot elongated apparatus that pulls the aircraft down the catapult track. Another deck handler under the plane, hooked up a trail bar that fit in behind the aircraft's front wheel assembly and interlocked into the catapult's zipper-track. The small tee fitting in front of the launch bar locked the aircraft into the forward part of the shuttle. At that time, the pilot could take his feet off the brakes, put his heels on the deck, while his upper foot stayed on the rudder pedals. The aircraft was locked into the catapult, therefore, it could not roll forward or backward. He was basically hooked up to the ship at this time, awaiting his

"Sling-Shot" propulsion down the cat track. The cat shot took the aircraft from zero knots to 160 plus knots in 1.8 seconds, causing about 4.5 G's on the pilot's body.

Once the aircraft was locked into the shuttle, the Yellow-Shirt passed the aircraft off to the Catapult Officer. For tonight's launch, Lt. Cmdr. Don "Super" Snyder would be launching aircraft off the bow catapults, one and two and Lt. Skip "Pretty-Boy" Floyd would be shooting the waist catapults, three and four.

The bright orange sky started to darken as night-fall began to settle over the Pacific. As the 1900 hour approached, the bow and angle deck safety lights turned from red to green. Looking at their watches, "Super" signaled to the Catapult green shirt under the plane to put catapult one into tension (like cocking a gun), as does the cat three officer. At that time, the CAG and Skipper Petriccione went to max power. Both catapult officers simultaneously raised one arm high in the air, with two fingers in a circling motion. The Pilot's wiped-out their cockpits by circling their control stick, which is mounted on the right side panel of the cockpit and simultaneously moved their rudders back and forth, checking all surfaces and instruments. Once satisfied all is a go, both pilots gave the CAT officers a sharp salute. As the second hand on the catapult officer's watches hits 1900 hours, the cat officers knelt forward and touched the deck with their high extended arms. This signal told the Green-Shirt Petty Officer in the starboard and port catwalks to fire the catapults, which released the built-up steam and hurled the aircraft down the deck. (One thing to note, if a pilot forgot to take his feet off the brakes, no worries, the plane would launch anyway; however, he'd blowout both tires, and end up with the nickname, "BOOM BOOM.")

Once the aircraft were airborne, the catapult officers would do the same procedure for cat's two and four. Launching the planes in this order allows plenty of separation between the aircraft and gets the planes off the deck quickly. Since there were only four planes on this launch, the cat officers wrapped up the catapults and made a ready deck, in case of an emergency if a plane needed to return to the ship early.

Once CAG's gear went up, he accelerated to 250 knots and climbed to 500 feet. Skipper Petriccione matched his speed and tucked up under his left wing. BigHands crossed under and behind the "Gunslinger Flight", and tucked himself under "Sweetwater's" right wing with fifteen inches of separation from wing-tip to nose. The "Big Bopper" pulled into the slot position, which was directly under Sweetwater and between Skipper Petriccione's aircraft and BigHands' plane, forming a tight diamond formation.

As the "Gunslinger Flight" approached Pt. Conception, Lt. Cmdr. Brown, who was in the slot position, eased back on his throttles and drifted behind the diamond formation. Once well clear, he added power and climbed his tanker F/A-18 to fifteen thousand feet and became the chase plane for the flight. CAG, looking to his left and right, gave the hand signal to his wingman to descend, then leveled the flight off at 400 feet AGL(above ground level). Once all aircraft were settled in and comfortable at 400 feet, he accelerated the flight to 350 knots and spread his wingmen out into a loose cruise position, which allowed them more time for visual lookout. After the aircraft spread out, his wingmen turned on their APG-81 radar . . .

By this time, it was almost dark and the lights started glistening in the surrounding towns. The DAS (Distributed Aperture System) in the F-35C made night time seem like daytime, which was an added feature to this new stealth aircraft.

As the formation neared "Jack Ass Flats", the night sky sparkled with stars, and the earth lit up the nearby town's city lights. The formation spread out, flying in a "loose goose" formation. It was smooth sailing until Sweetwater heard Petriccione scream, "Holy shit! Holy shit!" over the tactical frequency.

"What? What is it?"

"It's birds! Black birds!"

Petriccione's *Lightning* had come under attack by a large migration of black birds; there were so many that the space around him was blacker than the night sky itself.

"Shit! I'm hit! Dash-One is hit!" Petriccione yelled. "I'm losing power, climbing to five thousand feet!"

"Roger that." Sweetwater replied. "Dash-Two, how's your aircraft?"

Johnson replied, "I'm okay. I think I besmirched my flight suit though."

A chuckle escaped Matt. "Okay, stay spread, and keep me in sight. How you doin', Dash-One?"

"I'm killing snakes in the cockpit right now—I'll get back to you."

"Roger that."

After what seemed like an eternity, Petriccione radioed back. "Dash-One here, I'm alright. Everything's under control. Diverting to Lemoore."

"Roger, Dash-One. Stay safe."

Bopper came up on tactical, "I'll escort the Skipper back to Lemoore, I'll let you know when he's safely on the ground."

"Roger, we'll see you at the gas station after the fireworks," Sweetwater said. "Well Johnson, looks like it's just you and me."

"We're the dream team, right?"

"We're about to find out!"

The "Gunslinger Flight" climbed back up to 500 feet and continued on route. Dash-Two pulled in closer to CAG's airplane as they started going over the Tehachapi Mountain range. They hit "Jack Ass Flats" at 500 feet, 350 knots undetected and unloaded their weapons package on the targets. As they climbed to fifteen thousand feet, heading towards the Tehachapi Mountain Range where the "Bopper" was circling, they could see the column of trucks, buses, and tanks lit up like Christmas trees. Mission accomplished.

Before they continued on their flight path, they needed to refuel, and they got some in the air. CAG spotted the green rotating beacon under the F/A-18 re-fueling tanker, which was flying in a left-hand pattern and waiting for their rendezvous in the pitch black of the night. He and BigHands joined up in left hand echelon on Bopper's wing. When cleared in to tank, CAG went first and took on 1500 pounds of fuel, backed out of the refueling basket and moved to Bopper's starboard wing. Once stabilized,

Bopper cleared in BigHands. After BigHands completed tanking, he pulled straight out of the refueling basket and drifted back several plane lengths and then rejoined on CAG's right wing. After Bopper retracted the basket safely, he passed the lead to CAG, by using his flashlight and slipped back and down from CAG's aircraft. Once stable, he re-joined on CAG's left wing. The "Gunslinger Flight" then headed back to the ship, at fifteen thousand feet.

North of San Clemente Island, CAG checked in with Beaver Control and the ship as he entered W-291. At that time, CATCC (Carrier Air Traffic Control Center) gave the "Gunslinger Flight" marshaling instructions to land.

Once the planes were safely recovered onboard, they were chocked and chained by catapult one. CAG waited for BigHands and Bopper to join him on the flight deck. As they approached him, CAG gave them a big thumbs-up and patted them on the back, with the words, "shit hot job gents." At that moment, Capt. Morley, the ship's captain, came up on the 1MC and congratulated the "Gunslinger Flight" for a job well done, as they walked into flight deck control.

Later that evening, CAG received a knock on his state room door. He opened it to see his administrative chief standing there with a note for him.

"Good evening Chief, how's things going?"

"Couldn't be better, sir, everything is ship shape."

"What can I do for you?"

"Well, here's a message that just came over the wire from 3rd Fleet; I thought you'd want to see it."

"Thanks, Chief! I'll take a look at it. Have a good evening."

"Aye-aye sir," he replied, as he departed. Matt walked over to his rack (bed), sat down and opened the message that read; *"Congratulations on a successful CENTEX Operation. Carrier Strike Force Foxtrot is ready for deployment and Godspeed with Operation "Rolling Thunder."* Rear Admiral Coleman info:

He breathed a sigh of relief. The training was over. The battle was about to begin.

Out of the frying pan, and into the fire.

The next morning before the air wing flew off the ship and went back to their respective bases, CAG called Skipper Petriccione in his office. Capt. Petriccione knocked on CAG's door.

"Come on in, Nick; have a seat. I need to brief you on something."

"Yes Sir," replied the skipper.

'What I'm about to tell you is top secret and is not to be discussed with your squadron until we deploy. "Prior to work-ups I was involved in a compartmented meeting at Raven Rock, you know where that is, correct?"

"Yes, sir, but I've never been there."

"Well, your squadron's aircraft will be flying on a top secret mission called 'Rolling Thunder.' I've selected Lt. Johnson to be my wingman during this mission. After you depart I'm going to talk to BigHands about his involvement. He is going to be sent TAD (temporary additional duty) on the fly-off this morning to a base for training regarding the mission and he will not be back for ten days.

Prior to the fly-off today you'll need to have an AOM (all officers meeting) and brief need-to-know personnel that he's being sent TAD; orders from CAG. Make it absolutely clear to everyone that no one is to question Lt. Johnson as to where he's been and what's going down, understood?"

"Yes, sir", replied the skipper.

"When the timing is right everyone on the ship will learn about this mission. However, it is imperative right now that very few know all the details. We can't afford to have every sailor and officer talking about this mission until they need to know. You know what can happen, letters to family and phone calls that could leak out bits and pieces of valuable information, which could be intercepted and cause the mission to fail."

"Yes, sir, I understand perfectly."

At that point, there was a knock at the door. Chief Reid opened the door and said to CAG, "I have Lt. Johnson here waiting to see you, sir."

"Have him wait outside; I'll be just a minute," CAG ordered. And when the door was closed again, he spoke to the skipper.

"Nick, you know the drill, I'd brief you on the whole mission now if I could, however, my hands have been tied at the highest level."

"I understand fully what you need done CAG, consider it done."

"Thanks. Have a safe fly-off and we'll see you back aboard in several weeks."

"Roger that, thank you sir," Skipper Petriccione affirmed. He left CAG's office. As he exited, Lt. "BigHands" Johnson came to his attention and asked him, "Good morning, sir, am I in some sort of trouble?"

"No you're not, young man, but if you fuck up what CAG's about to brief you on, you won't be worth buffalo shit on a nickel."

"Roger that, Skipper!" He shouted out, as his eyes widened.

"Make your shipmates proud of you. I'll see you in a week or so."

BigHands gave him a bewildered look as he said, "Will do, Skipper." Then he entered CAG's office and closed the door behind him.

CHAPTER ELEVEN

THE PROFESSOR

"Good work out there today, guys. Great hustle." Bastos said as he ushered the University of Bushehr Soccer Team into the locker room. "You've all earned a rest. No practice tomorrow. Hit the books, and I'll see you all on Monday." The team cheered at the good news and filed past him.

"Ah, very impressive, Mohammed. I trust these boys are giving you no trouble?" Tayyib Al'Qim had snuck up behind him. Even hearing his voice caused the hairs on Bastos' back to rise. He quickly put on a smile and turned around.

"No Tayyib! These boys have done an excellent job. We'll be quite ready for the game next week." Bastos said.

Al'Qim nodded approvingly. "And your physics classes . . . they are going well, no?"

"Even better, in fact! The students are so incredibly smart. I wouldn't be surprised if they start teaching me pretty soon!" Tayyib laughed at that. "Well, let's hope for both our sakes, the students don't attempt a coup."

Tayyib's face grew serious. "Mohammed, enough of the small talk now. I have long pondered whether or not to tell you what I am about to tell you. Over the past few months that we've worked together, I have begun to view you as I would a son." Bastos' heart leapt. *This could be it. Have I finally earned his trust?* Quickly, he said. "Wow, that is such an incredible honor, to be viewed by you as a son."

"It is a privilege not many share. I have watched your work ethic, and our weekly Mahjong games have convinced me of one thing—you are a man who, above all else, values loyalty. And I view loyalty above all else. Come. I have something to show you."

Bastos stuttered out a "thank you" and followed Tayyib Al'Qim into his car. Al'Qim started the ignition and began to drive. "What I am about to show you is a world-changer, understand? Things of this nature are, of course, very secretive. I am only showing you this because I trust you. If you betray my trust, I can promise you this, you will never betray anyone else, ever again. Understood?"

Agent Miller nodded his head. "Understood. You have my word, Tayyib."

"Good."

After a drive that seemed like hours, they pulled into the parking lot of the Bushehr Nuclear Plant. Al'Qim drove his vehicle to the front of the building, into a parking spot that read "*Reserved.*"

"I have no doubt that you've seen this power plant, no?" Al'Qim said as they walked through the large double doors of the facility.

"Of course I have. It dominates the Bushehr skyline. I never dreamed that I would get to see the inside, and all the science that goes into this."

"Oh believe me, Mohammed, I know. This power plant . . . this is my legacy. This is what my children and grandchildren will remember me by." Tayyib turned around and looked at Bastos. "This is what the entire world will remember me by." He said with a slight smile.

He continued, "Construction of this power plant began, as I'm sure you know, in 1975 by a conglomeration of German companies. The plan was to give Iran a reliable source of power, but that was thwarted by the Islamic Revolution of Iran. After that, the unfinished building lay dormant for exactly twenty years." They began to enter the heart of the power plant itself. Bastos saw hundreds of workers in a truly extensive operation.

"In 1995, the Russians took over the project. They were never able to complete it, however. Financial difficulties as well as interference from the West has kept this beautiful building from fulfilling its true purpose."

"Its true purpose? What exactly is its true purpose?"

Tayyib smiled at him. "That is what brings us here today. In the span of one year, I did what the Germans and the Russians could not." He motioned to the bustle of the workplace below. "I gave Iran a weapon."

"A weapon?"

"Yes, my dear Mohammed. The mightiest weapon of all—fear." Tayyib smiled to himself.

"Fear? Tayyib, I'm not sure I understand."

"For far too long the West kept the East in bondage. How do they do this? With fear. Our children live in fear that their homes will be destroyed by American bombs, and that our cities and towns will be occupied by the United Nations. They come to us in the guise of 'peace keeping' but no, we know what they are here to do. They are trying to keep us under their thumb!" Tayyib was raising his voice, and he motioned for Bastos to follow.

"Mankind began in the East. We were the cradle of civilization! We should be leading the world, not them! For far too long have we dreamed of the day that we could take the world back, but it has always escaped our grasp. That is, until today."

Tayyib ushered Agent Miller into a locked, secure room. He flipped on the lights, and Bastos saw an astounding sight; maps, so many maps, each of them detailing an unspeakable strategy that portrayed the demise of the western civilization.

"This is our plan. Finishing the power plant was our first step. Iran is now on the path to becoming a nuclear power, the first nuclear power that will actually empower us with its new found capabilities."

Bastos examined a nearby map. It was of the Middle East, but there were no lines of division signifying different countries. It was all one color. He pointed to it, and said, "What is this? A unified Middle East?"

"Ah, yes! Imagine it—one nation that controls the majority of the oil on Earth! With the flip of a switch, we could bring the West crumbling to its knees. That, my dear Mohammed, is how we use fear."

"But how are you going to do this? Are the other countries just going to roll over and let you occupy them? What about Israel?"

"We have a few countries that have already pledged their allegiance to us; Iraq, Afghanistan, and Saudi Arabia, to name a few." Tayyib saw Bastos raise his eyebrow. "Oh yes, it's true. You didn't really think those countries were totally in America's pocket, did you? They'll join us when the time is right."

"As for Israel . . . well, we will show the world that we mean business. We will use our newly built nuclear arsenal to sink Israel to the bottom of the Dead Sea. And the West will do nothing to stop us because they know that we control their oil."

"After that, we'll kill the West slowly, and painfully." Tayyib smiled to himself. "We'll raise gas prices. Their economies will plummet, and their people will riot, and then revolt." With an air of confidence, Tayyib turned and faced Bastos. "The best part about this plan, my dear Mohammed? We won't have to raise a hand directly against the West. They will kill themselves for us."

Agent Miller was stunned. The facts were all laid out before him and Tayyib already had his trump card. The factory was already online and enriched uranium was already flowing in. If he was right about the other nations in allegiance with Iran, the situation was far worse than anyone could imagine.

"This plan, professor. This plan will change the world. I have to ask though . . . why are you showing me this?"

"You, Mohammed, are going to be my right hand man. Come December, the dignitaries from all the nations in the Middle East will be coming here to discuss the unification of the East, and the destruction of Israel. You will sit at my right hand, and you will help me convince any nay sayers. You have shown me your quality, and so I have deemed you worthy of this honor. Do you accept?"

Bastos stammered, "Y-yes! Absolutely. To sit at the

right hand of the man who will change the world? I can think of no better seat." Even as he said that, his head was spinning. "*December? That's so soon! We thought any kind of action would be at least a couple of years away, but Tayyib is already about to unleash his hell upon the world.*

"I'm glad to hear you say that, Mohammed. Truthfully, had you said no, I would have had to kill you, right here." Agent Miller tensed. But, Tayyib laughed, "Of course, we don't need to worry about that now, do we? For now, my dear friend we simply wait."

The last thing that Agent Miller was going to do was wait. That next day, on Thursday, Bastos was sitting in his usual spot out on the patio at Seray-Hammam, a café in Akhtar. His weekly game with Tayyib Al'Qim was scheduled to start in a few minutes, although his "friend" had yet to arrive. He looked at his watch. 1530. It was time the Argus satellite would be directly overhead, waiting for Agent Miller to relay any information he had gathered through the Mahjong cards. The first card that he threw face-up was the Nine of Circles, this meant immediate danger. He then put out the Five of Bamboo, which signified an imminent nuclear threat, followed by the Circle of One, which meant entirety of the Middle East. He then revealed the Four of Characters, followed by the Three of Bamboo, and the Seven of Circles. The men on the other end of the Argus understood Iran was planning on taking over the Middle East, and America and her allies were in grave danger, and that "Rolling Thunder" had to be executed in December.

Out of the corner of his eye, Agent Miller saw Tayyib

Al'Qim round the nearby corner. He quickly shuffled the cards back in his deck, and stood up to greet him.

"Ah, Mohammed! You beat me again! It's like you purposely get here before me!"

"It's not my fault, Tayyib! The coffee in this place is magnificent! I can hardly get through my classes on Thursday! All I think about is this delicious cup of caramel, sugar, cream and coffee."

Tayyib laughed, "Well, I'll give you that." As he sat down, he said, "So, are you ready to play?"

CHAPTER TWELVE

HAZE GRAY AND UNDERWAY

As Matt Sullivan stepped off the USS Ronald Reagan (CVN-76) onto the pier of Pearl Harbor, the memories of his grandfather began to rush back to him. He had taken Matt to Pearl Harbor before, when he was a kid. He showed Sweetwater where he and his squadron-mates lived, the hangars where they kept the planes, where they ate, and where he and his squadron-mate, Zac Taylor, narrowly escaped The Day That Would Live in Infamy. Matt let the sounds of the harbor fill his ears, and he allowed a moment of silence in honor of his grandfather, and the men who gave their lives in defense of this harbor and country.

Carrier Strike Force Foxtrot had spent the last two weeks transiting the Pacific from San Diego to Hawaii. They flew day and night across the pond and participated in RIMPAC (Rim-of-the-Pacific) in and around the Hawaiian Islands, with six foreign Navy units. This exercise was designed to hone the combat skills of the battle groups involved, in simulated war games in the air, on the surface and with submarines, throughout the Islands, before pulling into port for several days of liberty. This was the beginning of Carrier Strike Force Foxtrot's seven month deployment, that would eventually take them to the Persian Gulf and Operation "Rolling Thunder." This didn't mean, however, that the carrier strike group would just set sail instantly to the Persian Gulf—that would draw way too much attention. Instead, the CSF prepared for a journey that looked like a simple routine patrol throughout the world's oceans and the first stop was Pearl Harbor.

While Sweetwater was reminiscing about his grandfather, the crew and airwing sailors of the *Reagan* were ready and raring to get off the ship and raise some hell. After two plus weeks at sea, working around the clock during the RIMPAC war games, everyone was ready to light their hair on fire and paint the entire Hawaiian Islands red.

Many of the squadrons had already booked their hotel suites for their admin parties. For a year, prior to going on cruise, the officers contributed funds to pay for the different suites they'd stay at throughout the cruise. These suites always had a duty officer assigned around the clock, to watch the room. Squadron personnel could come and go, drop off gifts, clean up before hitting the bars and have some drinks while relaxing on the beaches of Waikiki.

The Gunslinger Squadron's admin, was located at the Sheraton Waikiki Hotel, right on the beach. Lt. BigHands Johnson was joined by Lt. j.g. "Rat" Anderson, Lt. "Hellcat" Ringer and Lt. "Moose" Mulligan. As they headed off the officer's brow with their liberty gear in their backpacks, they hailed one of the hundred taxis waiting to drive the *Reagan's* sailors to the beach. They booked a room at the Outrigger Regency away from the squadron's admin room. This would allow them their own space to relax without the noise of the continuous coming and going of other squadron-mates.

"Man, I cannot wait to tie one on and chase some pelt (women) tonight!" Rat Anderson said, as they hopped into their taxi and headed for the Outrigger.

The trip from Pearl Harbor to Waikiki beach took about twenty-five minutes depending on traffic.

Rat said to the driver, "Where is the closest package store where we can pick up some beer"?

"There's one right outside the gate," the driver replied.

"Great, please pull in." Rat looked over his shoulder at his shipmates. "We need a couple of six packs so we can get this party started!"

"Right on," they replied.

After their pit-stop, the junior officers, who were all on their first deployment, had already downed two six-packs by the time they'd reached the hotel. As they paid their cab fee, they felt the warm tropical breeze hit their faces and the fragrant smell of the plumeria flowers set the tone for a wild in-port period. Once they checked into their rooms, the pilots headed down to the beach to the Sheraton, where their admin suite was set up.

As they entered the suite, the party had already started, the music was loud, the alcohol was flowing, and the dancing girls had arrived. BigHands took one look at one of the dancers and said to himself, "Sweet Jeeezus" as he headed to the bar to get a Jack-on-the-Rocks.

"Mind if you make one for me?" A voice behind him said. Johnson turned around; it was Lt. Cmdr. Nicky Mathers.

"Nicky what are you doing here?" he asked.

"Our admin suite is a couple of floors down, but I could hear the noise up here from our balcony, so I decided to come up and see my favorite squadron, the Gunslingers," she said with a smirk on her face.

Since they were both "ring knockers"(naval academy graduates), the two began to socialize, and they talked about their careers.

On the other side of the bar, Rat, Hellcat and Moose were engaged in a drinking game.

"Al-alright you sonsofbitches, I can drink ya'll under the rug any day of the week!" As a fired-up Moose said. "Pour me another one!"

The three men were drinking tequila shooters and getting primed for an evening on the town. Usually the first night in-port was fairly wild, due to being cooped up on the ship for weeks.

Hellcat was sitting out on the suite's balcony looking at some information on Hawaii, when all of a sudden he came off the balcony and announced, "No one has a hair on their ass if they don't come with me tonight for a hula lesson! C'mon, who's in?"

"I'm in," Rat says, which was quickly followed by BigHands saying, "Count me in!" Moose was taking a combat nap; they'd drag him along whether he wanted to or not and several others said they would come as well.

BigHands looked at Nicky and asked, "Are you gonna join us?"

"No sorry, I've got plans. Say, I best get back to my squadron's party. See you guys around town. Stay out of trouble!" she said with a twinkle in her eye as she departed.

As more and more squadron-mates and other airwing

pilots stopped by, the suite started to get really crowded. BigHands grabbed Rat and Hellcat and said, "Let's go for a swim! After that, we'll head back to our hotel and get cleaned up for tonight's festivities."

The men nodded, but Hellcat asked, "What about Moose?"

"Ah, let him sleep it off! We'll catch up with him later."

The three Gunslingers changed into their swim gear and headed to the beach. After an hour of relaxing in the ocean and watching the "talent" stroll by, the guys headed back to their suite to get their backpacks, and to see if Moose was up.

As they headed into their suite, the youngsters ran right into Capt. Sullivan.

"Good Afternoon, CAG."

"Excuse me, I didn't see you standing there."

"No problem," CAG replied.

Sweetwater asked, "Enjoying yourself?"

"Yes sir! Like a fox in a henhouse."

Matt laughed. "That's great. Have fun, and be safe out there."

"Will do, sir!"

CAG was making his rounds to all his airwing suites to show his presence and support of all his men and women. Skipper Petriccione had also arrived at the suite and was having a few snaps with his squadron.

By this time Moose was back to earth and engaged with a few of the other squadron's females who had stopped by for a drink.

Hellcat grabbed him and said, "Come on, Moose, we're headed back to our hotel! We've got a big night lined up. Grab your shit and let's go, big guy."

"Alright, alright, I'm coming," he said as he offered a hasty goodbye to his female companions. With that, the gang headed to their rooms.

After they had showered and cleaned up, they headed to "The House Without a Key," the famous Halekulani Hotel. It was here, where Ms. Kanoe Miller (a former Miss Hawaii), was performing and she would give a hula session after her show to those who wanted to participate. While watching the show, the guys had some "snacks and courage", before they got up on stage and made complete asses of themselves. All in all, they had a great time and each got to have their picture taken with Kanoe.

After their hula lesson, BigHands and the guys headed out to a couple more bars to watch shows and mingle with the locals. As midnight approached, the guys decided it was time to get some shut eye and caught a cab back to their hotel. When they got to the lobby, it was hopping, so the guys went in for a nightcap.

The Outrigger Regency had a unique pool. While sitting in the lounge, listening to the entertainment, you could watch the guests swimming, through this huge glass window behind the bar.

After several drinks, the Gunslingers were back up on step again and Johnson said, "Gents, let's go for a swim"!

"A swim? In this pool?" Hellcat asked.

"Hell yeah!" Moose said. "It's a pool with windows instead of walls! Windows are the new thing, man. Get with the times."

"Guys. Guys! I just had the greatest idea ever," Rat said.

BigHands groaned. "That's never a good sign."

"Aw, c'mon man! Live a little, this will be awesome."

"For you, awesome usually translates to big trouble, but fine, I'll bite. What's your idea?"

"We . . . should moon the people in here from the pool."

"What?"

"Yeah! Moon people from the pool! You know, drop our suits? Let the world see the moon come up over the Outrigger!"

"You're fucking nuts," Johnson said. "We'll get our asses thrown in jail."

With a mischievous grin, Rat retorted with, "That's only if we get caught."

After they finished their drinks they went to their rooms and changed into their swim gear, came back and jumped into the pool. There were only several others in the pool at that hour.

"Alright, you guys ready?"

BigHands had no idea how they talked him into it, but there he was, swimming in the pool, down by the glassed-in area.

"I can't believe we're doing this," he said,

"C'mon! It'll be fun!" Moose said.

"One," said Rat.

"Two." BigHands tensed up.

"Three." *Well, it's too late to back out now,* thought Johnson.

"Go!" With that, the four men dove under the water, dropped their suits and pressed their asses against the window that was behind the bar. They could only imagine the gasps and people laughing hysterically inside.

Hellcat was the first to pull up his suit and as he surfaced, he could hear; "Security! Someone call security on these jackasses!"

Rat wanted them to hold their pressed hams for several more seconds, but Moose didn't wait. *I'm outta here. I'm fucking out of here!* he thought to himself as he booked it out of the pool.

"Ah shit!" said BigHands, as he surfaced, pulling his suit up and swimming towards the right side of the pool. He saw Hellcat heading towards their room as he was climbing out of the pool.

The other mooners grabbed their towels and flew upstairs to their room.

They rushed inside and locked the door. The four pilots looked silently at each other for a moment, and then burst out laughing.

"Did you see those faces on the people in the bar?"

"They about shit themselves when we dropped our suits! They had no idea what to do!"

"Security! Someone call security!" Rat said in a mocking tone. "What's security going to do?"

"Man, that was a blast!" BigHands said. "Maybe I should listen to you guys more."

"Damn right you should!" said Moose.

"For now, we celebrate. Let's have a nightcap," said Rat, as he pulled a cold bottle of tequila out of the small fridge.

Before he could pour the drinks, there was a loud knock at the door. The four went zip-lipped. Three more knocks followed. Then, a yell: "Security! Open up this door! Right now!"

"Fuck," said Moose.

"No, no, it's okay, we got this. They have no proof!" said Rat. He opened up the door. A member of the hotel's security was on the other side. "Good Evening, sir, what can I do you for?"

"What unit are you gentlemen in?"

"Ah, The Gunslingers VFA-105, sir. Can I ask what this is about?"

"Well, you classy gentlemen deemed it necessary to show the world your asses in the pool."

"Our asses? No sir, that was not us. We've been up here all night!"

"All night?"

"Yes, sir!" said Rat.

"How do you explain the trail of wet carpet that leads to your room, then? And why are you all still soaking wet?"

". . . shit." said all four of them.

"Pack up your gear gentleman, the shore patrol is on its way, they'll be taking you back to the ship. The hotel manager is not going to file charges, however, a report will be sent to your commanding officer."

When the shore patrol showed up, they asked who the senior man was. BigHands raised his hand.

"Understand you're with VFA-105, is that correct?"

A sheepish, "Yes, sir" came from Johnson's mouth.

"And the others? Are they from the same squadron?"

"Yes sir," BigHands replied.

"Alright then, we're done here. Pay for your bill, and we'll be taking you back."

As the pranksters filed out from the lobby, the hotel manager broke out in laughter.

As the officers walked up the brow escorted by the shore patrol, they knew they were in a world of brown. The OOD (Officer of the Deck) and their executive officer (XO) Cmdr Bjarne Christensen met them as they reported back aboard. The shore patrol turned them over to their XO as they departed.

"Well, well, well, gents; it didn't take you guys long to screw up your three days of liberty, did it?"

They all replied in unison, "No, sir."

"Hmmph. I'm putting you in HACK (confined to the ship) However, I'm not confining you to your quarters. There is enough work that needs to be done in and around our squadron to keep you guys busy for the next few days. The skipper will deal with you upon his return to the ship prior to getting underway. Understood?"

"Yes, sir," they replied.

The night before the ship sailed, all four of the party animals were standing tall in the CO's state room. Skipper Petriccione ripped them all a new asshole and confined them to the ship for the first day in-port while in Singapore, the next port of call. He dismissed Rat, Hellcat and Moose, but told BigHands to stand by. After the others departed the room, the skipper really laid into Lt. Johnson

"Goddamn it, Gary! What in the hell were you thinking?"

Knowing to keep his pie hole shut, Johnson just said, "No excuse, sir."

You're goddamn right there's no excuse! You're my number one JO (junior officer) and you have been selected for a highly sensitive mission and I wouldn't be surprised if, after this stunt, CAG doesn't find someone else!"

"Don't worry, sir, I won't—" before he could say another word, the skipper told him to shut his mouth.

For the next several minutes he continued his verbal assault, then excused him. As BigHands exited the stateroom, you could almost see the chunk of his ass that had been removed from his butt.

CHAPTER THIRTEEN
CHRISTMAS PACKAGES ARRIVE

"Well, Buck, you did it. You're an honorary SEAL member now. Kick-ass job, Marine." Cmdr. Bowman said, giving Savage a strong handshake. "It looks like we're shipping out soon. We're meeting up with Strike Force Foxtrot off Diego Garcia."

"Thank you, sir. It's an absolute honor to be an honorary member of the most elite fighting force in the world."

"You've earned it, Buck. Believe that," Pig said. "Your DDS training is complete. Take this weekend to relax, but be back here at 0500 sharp on Monday. We'll be flying out to Diego Garcia to get this show on the road."

"Yes, sir!"

Buck spent that weekend mostly in solitude. He was mentally preparing himself for the challenge that he would have to face. The enormous pressure that he was under was beginning to get to him, and he had to keep it in check. *If I miss that shot, we lose. I only get one chance—there will be no do-overs. This one shot, hit or miss, will change the world.* He spent his time disassembling and reassembling the BLR Lightning rifle; he already knew the gun inside and out, but more training wouldn't hurt!

That Monday, Buck and the Red Squadron from SEAL Team Six, headed out to Diego Garcia via a C-17 military transport aircraft. When they arrived on Fantasy Island (Diego Garcia) itself, there was no rest for the wicked.

Carrier Strike Force Foxtrot steamed out of Pearl Harbor and made a bee line for the South China Sea. The aircrews flew their day and night sorties to stay qualified; there was no time to waste in transit. Due to intelligence and updated information, the time frame for "Rolling Thunder" had a very small window of opportunity.

The *Reagan* was supposed to spend five days in Singapore, however, their in-port period was cut short. The stop was basically for diplomatic purposes and to take on fresh stores. Sweetwater sent Dr. Farrio a message prior to entering port, explaining the short turn-around in Singapore, and that it would be better to meet in Dubai. Once in port, Matt talked with Mary and they made arrangements to rendezvous in the UAE (United Arab Emirates), where they could spend cherished time together. Although disappointed, Mary agreed and started arranging her new travel plans. BigHands and the other mooners, never got off the ship to set foot on Singapore soil due to the short stay.

The port call in Singapore was a whirlwind visit, especially for the senior officers. There were many meetings and communications with the Pentagon, plus updating timelines for "Rolling Thunder". Singapore is one of the busiest ports in the world and it's one of the smallest countries, area wise. With Strike Force Foxtrot in town, the city was extremely crowded. One could hardly get a Singapore Sling at The Raffles Hotel without waiting for fifteen minutes.

After two days in-port, the carrier strike group left Singapore and headed through the Straits of Malacca, the busiest shipping lane in the world, sailing into the Arabian Sea. Once safely out of the narrow straits, the small-boy ships and sub steamed for the Gulf of Oman, while the carrier headed down toward Diego Garcia. The *Reagan* was steaming 30 plus knots till they got within COD (carry onboard delivery) range of Diego Garcia. When the ship was 400 miles east of "Fantasy Island", the C-2 Greyhound aircraft was fired off the deck. At that time, the carrier turned around and headed for the Gulf of Oman to join back-up with the strike force. It took Santa Claus about five hours to pick up his Christmas packages and return to the ship.

The COD landed aboard around two in the morning, when most of the ship's crew were sleeping. The mission was planned that way, so there would be very little attention as to what was being brought on board. The aircraft trapped aboard at 0215 and was chocked and chained abreast of the Carrier's Island, just forward of the number three wire.

The Clam-Shell doors opened and the aircraft shut down. Rear Admiral Coleman, Capt. Morley and CAG, met the packages as they filed out the back of the air-craft. Cmdr. Bowman saluted the three and requested permission to come aboard (Navy Protocol). The salute was returned by Rear Adm. Coleman, and they were immediately escorted to the Admiral's conference room.

The weapons officer, Commander Bob Adler and his "Weps" crew off-loaded the two main Christmas packages from the aircraft and stored them below deck in the weapon's magazines. This new "CHAMP" Missile was a "Counter Electronics High Power Microwave Advanced Missile"; capable of shutting down all electrical power within a ten mile radius.

Lt. "BigHands" Johnson was sent TAD to Kirkland Air Force Base in New Mexico, before deployment. His F-35C *Lightning* aircraft was retrofitted to carry and launch this missile, at selected targets. Lt. Johnson fired this weapon several times on the Utah missile range with deadly results. He was the first pilot to actually fire this missile from an aircraft and he was the only STICK (pilot) qualified to do so.

As the Red Squadron team sat around the Admiral's conference table, his head steward brought Cmdr. Bowman and his men a cup of coffee. Admiral Coleman sat at the head of the table, welcomed everyone aboard and got right down to business. "Gentleman, while aboard, you're going to be assigned to the weapons department. Your cover is as follows; you've come from the USS Princeton (CG59) which is in our Strike Force Foxtrot to do some weapons training. Once we pull out of Dubai, the whole crew will be brought up to speed on our "Rolling Thunder" mission."

"Gunny Buck, you may not know this, but the Taliban has put a two million dollar bounty on your head." The now-bearded Buck Cassidy nodded. "I'm glad to see your facial growth is filling in, you may need this disguise while on your kill mission. I cannot emphasize how delicate this operation is going to be. Everyone needs to be full on, because each one of you is a major link in the success of this mission. If one of the links breaks down, we'll not achieve our ultimate goal. Am I being perfectly clear?"

Everyone replied, with a "Yes, sir."

"We'll join the rest of the strike force within a couple of days and we'll operate in the Gulf of Oman for several days before we pull into Dubai. Go about your business as usual, fit into our schedule and avoid any direct questioning you may receive from others on the ship. And remember: you're TAD from the *Princeton* to get weapons training.

"Capt. Morley, CAG; do you have anything to add?"

"No sir," they replied.

"Okay men, my steward will assign you your berthing areas. It's been a long day for everyone, get some sleep and enjoy your stay while on the *Reagan*. Always remember; *when we fight, we will win.*"

They all came to attention and the Admiral dismissed the group.

CHAPTER FOURTEEN
LIBERTY CALL DUBAI

The Reagan joined the rest of the strike force as they reached the Gulf of Oman. The carrier carried out normal operations while in the area. The Princeton towed a bombing sled for the aircraft to practice their skills on and the weapons department deployed small targets off the fantail of the carrier so Buck and others could keep their shooting accuracy in check.

Since the carrier left Singapore, the crew had been at sea almost a month and everyone was ready for some well-deserved liberty. However, before the ship pulled into port, Skipper Morley reminded the crew of the *USS Reagan* that he'd received a message from King Neptunus Rex, Ruler of the Deep, that all Slimy "Pollywogs"(novices) onboard his vessel would not escape the "Crossing the Line" Ceremony. When the carrier crossed at Latitude 00-00, Longitude 75.2 E on its way to Diego Garcia, the Ruler of the Raging Main, made it clear, that he would visit the *USS Ronald Reagan* and the "Crossing the Line" tradition, so ancient that its origins predate written history, would be carried out. Therefore, the *Reagan* would only have trusty Shellbacks onboard when the ship returned to

San Diego from its deployment. The carrier and its escort ships arrived in Dubai at 0900 on the 28th of November. They would pull out of port on the afternoon of December 2nd, the day Dubai with Abu Dhabi and five others would gain their independence from the UK.

Matt had been so busy since leaving San Diego, he really didn't have time to think about his best friend Boomer that had gone missing just before he deployed. While gathering his clothes and packing his bags for a romantic visit with Mary, he had a sinking feeling as he looked at a picture of Boomer and himself fishing at Mammoth Lake. The sadness was interrupted when a knock came on his stateroom door, it was Chief Reid.

"Good Morning, Chief, what can I do for you?"

"Sir, your presence is required in the Admiral's conference room at eight."

"Thanks, Chief, I'll be there."

"Roger that, sir," he said, as he shut the door.

As he continued to pack, Matt thought to himself, *Now what could all this be about?*

By the time Matt got down to Admiral Coleman's conference room, it was packed. Skipper Morley, Cmdr. Bowman and his crew, Gunny Buck, Capt. St. John, the *Michigan's* Commanding Officer, and the weapons officer were all seated around a large green velvet conference table.

"Gentleman, thanks for gathering on such short notice. I received a FLASH message from the Pentagon early this morning. It stated that things have heated up in Iran and they want "Rolling Thunder" to be activated on December Seventh. Everyone in this room knows what

I'm talking about. This mission will go down in the history books and, as such, failure is not an option. Understand?"

A loud "Aye, Aye Sir," was bellowed back at the Admiral.

"We have several days to get our batteries charged while in this beautiful city. Go out and have fun, but be ready to go to war when we pull out on the second. Oh yes, one more thing. There will be no communication with the outside world once we leave port. This means, there will be no mail calls, no calls off the ship and no messages sent until "Rolling Thunder" has been completed. I'll brief the rest of the strike force CO's tomorrow at our morning briefing. Are there any questions?"

The room was silent. "Okay then, let's go have some fun."

Everyone came to attention and they were dismissed.

Matt headed back to his stateroom and finished packing. By the time he had gathered up his gear, the liberty boats had arrived and the ship's crew was beginning to disembark. There was a big barge anchored by the fantail with a long gang plank that reached up to the ship's hangar deck; all personnel on the ship would use that as their exit and entry point.

As Matt walked down the steep gang plank to the barge, he began to think about Mary and what the next few days would bring. The liberty boats were huge and very modern looking, nothing like the Star Ferries in Hong Kong. The ride to shore took only ten minutes; the drinks and service en-route were impeccable.

Sweetwater had most of the details laid out for Mary

before she arrived. He had booked a room at the Burj Al Arab Hotel, a sailboat shaped tower that had the opulence and reputation of one of the world's finest five star hotels. It was a bit pricy at 2000 United Arab Emirates Dirhams (AED) a night, which equated to $740 US dollars. However, the hotel management lowered their prices for the strike force, which made it much more affordable for a senior officer.

The pier where the ferries off-loaded the ship's crew was a short taxi ride to the hotel. It was a little past noon when Matt arrived at the front entrance. He paid his cab fare and was heading towards the hotel when Mary came running out to greet him.

She threw her arms out to hug him and almost knocked him down when she jumped into his lap and wrapped her legs around his waist. They kissed passionately, as they blocked much of the entrance way into the hotel. When they both caught their breath, Mary couldn't stop holding Matt close to her, telling him how much she'd missed him. Matt wanted to reciprocate his feelings, but was so awestruck by her beauty that he couldn't get the words out of his mouth.

Once they both calmed down, Mary said, "I have a great surprise for you." Matt's face lit up like a Roman candle.

Mary laughed, "I know what you're thinking, you horny little devil and yes, that's going to be dessert. But first, we're going to have High Tea in the Sky View Bar, which is on the top floor of this magnificent hotel."

Matt had other plans on his mind, but didn't want to seem overly aggressive. Mary grabbed his hand and said,

"Come on! Let me show you our gorgeous room. Then, you can clean up and we'll head up to the Sky View Bar."

Sweetwater squeezed her hand. "Sounds great, young lady, lead the way."

When Mary opened the door to their suite, Matt could only say, "Wow!"

Mary smiled, "I know, right? What a view. It's breath-taking, isn't it?"

"Boy, it sure is," replied Sweetwater.

After a quick shower and a change of clothes, Matt was ready for High Tea. He actually never had High Tea with anyone, but knew what the drill was all about. Mary and Matt sat and got reacquainted while they sipped on tea, ate some sandwiches, and split several exotic pastries. After they were pleasantly full, they retreated to their beautiful suite on the 20th floor and consummated their reunion.

Once the voluptuous sexual encounter subsided and Matt's eyes cleared; the two love-birds showered and ordered room service for their evening meal and just relaxed in their room. The next day Mary had signed them up for the blue route, Dubai's hop-on-hop-off bus tour. It made 19 stops throughout the entire city, and they saved the best stop for last, the Dubai Mall. As one might imagine, it was a whirlwind tour that lasted all day. By the time the couple returned to their hotel, it was five pm. Matt and Mary headed to their room to drop off their treasures and clean up.

"Matt? I'm thinking about taking a bubble bath. Would you like to join me?" Mary asked.

"Well, hell yeah I would! I just need to make a few

calls, and then I'll join you. But first, shall I draw your water, Ms. Mary?" he said with a wink.

Mary smiled at him. "That would be lovely, Mr. Sullivan, thank you.

Matt, turned on the water, ensured the temperature was right and added the magic bubbles.

While Matt was looking up some numbers, Mary slipped off her robe as she walked past him. Her pert nipples were standing straight up, which caused Matt to immediately come to attention. He dropped his day-time planner on the floor. Mary motioned with her finger in a seductive manner, which excited Matt even more. Forgetting about the call, Matt followed her into the tub for yet another round of uncontrollable passion.

Once the water stopped bubbling, Matt hopped out and opened a bottle of champagne. He poured them each a glass and then set the bottle on the window side of the tub. They sat in the tub facing each other, discussing life issues, their future together and what was in store for the rest of the cruise.

After several glasses of bubbly, Matt had to be careful what he talked about, so he changed the subject quickly by saying; "My, my, these legs are quite stubbly. I think Dr. Sweetwater needs to get out his famous leg shaving kit and smooth these wheels up, what do you say?"

"I'd be honored," Mary said as she smiled. With that note, Matt filled her glass, got out of the tub and gathered his shaving instruments.

He set the razor and shaving cream on the side of the tub, along with a pair of cuticle scissors. Mary piped up and asked, "What are those for?"

"Don't worry my dear, I'll show you later. Just lay back, sip your champagne and relax; you're in the good hands of Dr. Sweetwater now."

Mary looked up at him and asked, "You won't cut me, right?"

"No ma'am, I've shaved over two thousand set of legs over the years and haven't had one scratch yet."

"Bullshit," Mary said with a laugh.

"No really! You see, it's all about the angles."

"What are you talking about?"

"Well, think about it; when you're bent over shaving your legs, your ankles, knee-caps and lower legs are hard to shave without cutting yourself, due to the angles. When I shave your legs, the angles aren't as steep; therefore, I can ensure a smooth clean shave. Trust me—I'm a professional."

Mary laughed again, "You're so full of shit, Sweetwater! It's okay though, because you make me laugh."

Matt gave her a wink. "Baby, just be calm now and enjoy Sweetwater's Spa Special."

After twenty minutes of pampering, Sweetwater had her legs as smooth as a newborn baby's butt. Mary was very relaxed and a little tipsy from the champagne and couldn't believe what a wonderful job he had done.

"Okay, Missy, it's time to hop in the shower and rinse off."

"Man, I don't think I can move! I'm so relaxed," replied Mary.

"Come on, I'll help you up," said Matt as he grabbed her arms.

While Mary was stabilizing herself, Matt turned on

the shower and picked up the cuticle scissors. Mary saw the scissors and asked, "What are you up to now? Are you going to perform surgery?"

Matt gave her a sly smile. "Well, you could look at it that way."

As they stepped into the shower, Matt asked, "Would you like a heart or a diamond design in your pubic area?"

Mary started to laugh hysterically. "You truly are nuts!"

"That's probably true! But I'm serious! You're getting the full Sweetwater treatment right now."

Mary gave him a seductive smile. "Well then, a diamond. I love diamonds." Being that Ms. Mary was quite hairy, it made for an easy design. Before she knew it, she had acquired a beautiful pubic hair diamond, well shaped and shaved.

While Mary was drying off, Matt made a call to the States to see if the Flintom's had heard anything about Boomer. San Diego was eleven hours behind Dubai time so it was only 0830 in the morning there. The phone rang several times and Carrie answered.

"Good morning, this is Dr. Flintom."

"Good morning, Carrie, this is Matt Sullivan in Dubai."

"Hi, Matt, good to hear from you. How is the deployment going?"

"It's going well, thank you. I called to see if you or Rob had heard anything regarding Boomer?"

"No, sorry, Matt. We had a couple of calls, but they didn't pan out. We're doing everything we can though. I know this must be hard on you."

"If you would, please continue to run the lost dog ad

and ensure it's in your veterinary bi-monthly newspaper."

"I sure will and if he shows up, we'll be sure to get a message to you."

"Thanks Carrie, give my best to Rob." Matt hung up and finished drying off.

Mary tried to console Matt, knowing he was hurting inside. Matt snapped back to reality quickly and said to Mary, "Let's just find a quiet place to have dinner and then call it a night."

"That sounds marvelous. You know, I'm pretty drained after today's merry-go-round," Mary said as she smiled. The two had a candle-light dinner in a nearby restaurant and were in bed by ten.

The next day was pretty subdued. The two relaxed in bed until noon, and they mostly stayed around their hotel. They swam in the magnificent pool, had a light dinner and went to bed early. The next morning, Matt and Mary had a quiet breakfast in their room. Matt packed his gear and got ready to head back aboard the ship to start preparing for "Rolling Thunder".

Matt had really fallen for Mary and it was difficult to say goodbye to her. He really never allowed anyone to get close to his inner soul, except Boomer. However, Mary was very different. She was smart, independent and sly like a fox, which made her so appealing. The taxi ride to the pier was pretty somber, not much talking, just holding hands and hugging. As the cab pulled up, the tears started to flow down Mary's face.

Matt pulled Mary close and gave her a tender kiss. "I love you, Mary, so much. I'll be seeing you soon."

She looked up at Matt with her big brown eyes and

said, "I love you, Matt Sullivan. I'll be waiting for your safe return."

Matt gave Mary another big hug and a kiss, and then headed towards the liberty boat that was about to depart. Before he boarded, he turned around and blew Mary a kiss. She caught it, and held it to her heart.

Within hours, the 20 ton anchors on the *USS Ronald Reagan* broke the water's surface and the sea and anchor detail prepared the ship for getting underway. Once the anchors were stored, you could hear the bos'n pipe blowing and the order came over the ship's 1MC. "Ships underway, shift colors". The deck department took the jackstaff down from the carrier's stern and moved the National Ensign (Flag) to the ship's super structure.

Once the ship hit the open ocean and began steaming into the Persian Gulf, Captain Morley came up on the ship's 1MC (as did the rest of the strike force's commanding officers).

"Now hear this! All hands aboard the *USS Ronald Reagan*; STAND TO AND LISTEN UP." Sweetwater was at his desk, pouring over tactical notes, and Gunny Buck was in the mess hall having coffee. The voice over the intercom continued, "On December 7th, Carrier Strike Force Foxtrot will initiate an attack on the Bushehr Nuclear Power Plant. This attack will occur under the cover of darkness. CAG and his wingman will attack and destroy parts of the nuclear power plant, sending a message to the Iranian government, that if they continue to enrich uranium for purposes other than producing energy, the plant will be completely destroyed at a later date. The new CHAMP missile which is a Counter Electronics High

Power Microwave advanced missile (EMP) will shut down the city of Bushehr's electricity and CAG, flying the F-35C *Lightning*, will then deliver four 1,000 pound bombs on the plant itself." The crew began to whoop and holler.

Skipper Morley continued, "While this is happening, Gunnery Sergeant Buck Cassidy will be strategically located and assassinate Tayyib Al'Qim, the mastermind behind the Bushehr Nuclear Power Plant. LIGHTNING WILL STRIKE TWICE, by air and on land. This will happen within minutes of each other, and it is paramount that our plan be kept secret. From this point on, and until "Rolling Thunder" has been successfully carried out, there will be no mail, no COD deliveries, and no off-ship communications."

"We're getting ready to go into "Harms Way," shipmates; stay sharp, be professional, do your jobs and remember, when Strike Force Foxtrot fights, we WIN. That is all. This is the captain, OUT."

CHAPTER FIFTEEN

TARGET ZONE

The winter honor suite.
The seven of bamboos.
The eight of characters.

Agent Miller was sitting at his usual spot at the Seray-Hammam cafe, and he was using the Mahjong deck to communicate with the Argus satellite. With those three cards, he had just told the crew on the other end of the Argus that "Rolling Thunder" had to occur on December 7th, at 1800. There was no other way around it; the strike had to happen then, or not at all. Three days left. That's all there was.

Bastos shuffled the cards back into the deck as he awaited Tayyib Al'Qim's arrival. The two had been playing Mahjong at this cafe since Agent Miller arrived in Iran, and in a fitting way, this is where it would all end. As he saw Tayyib turn the corner, he stood up to greet him.

"Ah, Dr. Al'Qim! How are you today?"

"I'm doing excellent, Mohammed. Can you feel it? Change is in the air! There's an energy in the very wind, like the earth itself knows that there is about to be a change in command." The two men shook hands, and they both sat down. Bastos began to shuffle the deck. "So how are you feeling, Mohammed? We will meet with the dignitaries at this very spot in three days. The world, as we know it, will be virtually transformed."

"I won't lie to you, Tayyib. I'm nervous. The weight of the world is on my shoulders. This is not something that I have taken lightly, it is the greatest of honors, but that doesn't mean it is without stress," Bastos said.

Tayyib laughed. "Of course there is stress! We are about to shift the power in the world, to bring the West to her knees. If it was easy, it would have been already done by now. But, my son, look at me." Agent Miller stared into his dark green eyes. "I would not have asked you if I did not believe in you."

The two men began to play the game. "Thank you, Tayyib. I am very grateful. I just want to do the best that I can."

"It is perfectly alright, Mohammed. For now though, let's go over the plan, shall we?" Bastos nodded. "The dignitaries will all gather at this very cafe at 1730, under the simple guise of a group of men meeting for a cup of coffee," he said.

"Okay," Bastos said." From there, we will proceed to tell them of our plan, in intricate detail. We will tell them about the power plant, about the nuclear power, and about our deliberate scheme to strangulate the flow of oil to the West."

"That in itself should convince the dignitaries of the merits of our plan. If we in the Middle East pledge our loyalties in agreement, the rest of the world will be rendered powerless to change it," Bastos said.

"Exactly! Whoever controls the oil, whoever controls the Middle East rules the world," Tayyib said. "For the first time in history, the East will control the Middle East. And we will watch the West beg."

"We should look at the other alternative, what if they say no?" Bastos asked. "What if some of them don't want to be a part of it?"

"That would be an unlikely scenario, for sure," said Tayyib, "considering our overwhelming evidence, but I see your point. Our rebuttal is simple; Iran's military, and the military coalition of the East will not suffer cowards. If they do not join us peacefully, we will force them to by other persuasive means. This is no time for half measures," said Tayyib.

"No time indeed," Bastos agreed.

The two men finished up their game, with Tayyib Al'Qim beating Agent Miller.

"Ah, Mohammed. Once again, I perceived your strategy before you could execute it. It would help to remember that a well thought out plan is made impotent if your opponent figures it out beforehand. There is an old saying . . . 'All warfare is based on deception.' The same could be said for Mahjong."

Bastos shuffled the deck and placed the cards in a carrying case. "Right you are, Tayyib. The same could be said for many things. Wait until next week. I'll show you just how deceptive I can be."

As Agent Miller walked into his apartment, he let out a sigh of relief. *Alright, I'm on the home stretch. Just three more days, and then Tayyib gets eliminated and I can head home.* He walked over to the fridge and pulled out a half-eaten sandwich. He walked around the apartment as he ate, surveying his surroundings.

This apartment is the place from where Buck "Savage" Cassidy would make his kill shot. Bastos thought it might be too obvious, but the location was just too perfect to pass up. *His balcony faces directly towards the Seray-Hammam cafe, and the complex itself is hidden behind a row of buildings and trees, so Buck would have ideal cover for his shot.*

Everything was planned out, even down to the seating arrangement. *Bastos will sit in his usual spot, his chair viewing the ocean. Tayyib Al'Qim would sit facing the road that was in front of the cafe. This way, the bullet from Buck's gun would pass along the side of Bastos' head right into Tayyib Al'Qim's skull, keeping Agent Miller safe from any bullet shrapnel or the exit wound. Once the kill shot was made, Buck and Bastos would haul ass out of Bushehr, and out of Iran.*

Craig Miller smiled as he took another bite of his sandwich. "Deception, Mr. Al'Qim?" He said aloud to himself. "Oh, I'll show you deception."

CHAPTER SIXTEEN
THE TRANSFER

"Alright ladies, this is it. Welcome to the big show!" Wiz said as SEAL Team Six's Red Squadron and Gunny Buck entered the motor-whale boat. "This is what we've all been waiting for." The men were headed towards the USS Michigan, which was the submarine that had been patrolling the Persian Gulf with Strike Force Foxtrot.

"It's about time! I've been itching to do this mission for months!" Maggot said, as he climbed into the boat.

"You ready, Savage? This is your big day," asked Wiz with a grin.

"Ready as I'll ever be. I'm just ready to get that bastard between my crosshairs."

Maggot laughed. "Yeah well, you know how life is in the military. 'Hurry up and wait!'"

"For you, Maggot, the military motto should be 'hurry up and shut up'." Hawk said as he climbed in. The rest of the men laughed.

"Yeah yeah, laugh all you want. Don't hate me because I'm beautiful. Which, speaking of beautiful things, look at that submarine!"

The *USS Michigan* was floating on the top of the water

directly beside the *USS Ronald Reagan*. The carrier itself dwarfed the sleek, black submarine, but the men couldn't deny just how striking the *Michigan* was.

"Damn she's a beauty," Said Hawk.

"Yeah, she sure is. Although, I'd like her a whole lot more if she wasn't just one tiny corridor," said Buck.

"Tiny corridor? This thing is huge! Length-wise, I mean." said Maggot incredulously.

"Is that how you convince women to sleep with you? It's not tiny, it's huge!'" said Hawk, which caused Buck and Wiz to burst out laughing.

"Yeah well, your mom didn't seem to mind."

"Alright, gentlemen, that's enough!" said Commander Tommy "Pig" Bowman as he stepped into the boat. "Play time's over; it's time to go to work."

"Yes sir!" they all said in unison.

With that, the ship's boatswain's mate took up the helm of the motor-whale boat, and motored over to the submarine itself. He stopped the tiny boat parallel to the massive war machine. Bowman said,"Alright men, grab your gear and head on up the sail and into the sub." The Red Squadron team quickly gathered their equipment and boarded the sub.

The *USS Michigan* had been in service for over thirty years, having been launched on her maiden voyage in 1980. As old as she was though, she was still a powerhouse to be reckoned with. The inside of the sub was cramped, and there were a few odors that Buck wasn't used to, but he acclimated quickly.

"Don't get too comfortable gentleman, we're making our way to the SHED right now. This way," Bowman said, as he led the SEAL team and Buck down the length of the sub to where the hatch was that lead to the DDS. They opened the hatch into the SHED, loaded their gear in and attached their equipment to the sled, the bar that would extend out on the top of the submarine.

"Once they've flooded the DDS . . ." Buck attached his gear inside the Zodiac which was tethered to the sled.

Tommy Bowman continued, "The Zodiac will be ready to go, once I've flooded. We'll then pull the sled out of the SHED and release the Zodiac on its tether. When it's aloft, Wiz, Hawk, and Buck will do a blow and go to the surface, Maggot you'll stay here to assist me. Understood?"

"Yes sir!" they all said.

"Easy and simple. Just like our training." Wiz said.

Once their gear was secured on the sled, Bowman said, "Nice work gents. Take a breather, explore the sub if you want, but get some sleep. Tomorrow, we plunge the battle into the bowels of hell."

"Yes sir!"

Buck didn't get much sleep that night. He didn't go exploring the submarine; he was much more contented to stay in his assigned rack. Thoughts of the mission kept running through his mind. *Why am I so nervous?* He thought to himself. *I've done high stakes ops before, but nothing has shaken me like this one has.* He sat up from his rack and scratched his head. *It's this fucking SHED that's got my mind coiled up tighter than a cinched rope. Damn Buck, just relax! You've been through this drill hundreds of times, so smile like a clam at high tide,* Buck thought to himself as he lay back down. The swabbie in the rack next to Buck made a wise crack about a Marine on a sub, which didn't sit well with Buck. He kept his piehole shut, so as not to start a pissing contest this late in the mission.

During the rest of the night and the next day, The USS Michigan had moved within five miles from where the crew would depart the Sub. At 2000 Buck and the SEALs were ready to make their ascent. All of the men had on scuba gear, and Commander Tommy Bowman gave the count down on his fingers.

Five.
Four.
Three.
Two.
One.

With that, he pulled the pressurized lever on the DDS, and began to flood the SHED. When the room was completely flooded, Hawk and Maggot opened the outer doors of the DDS and swam out. They released the locking mechanism on the sled and pulled it out of the SHED on its rail. They unhooked the Zodiac along with the gear, still attached by the tether to the sled and sent the equipment to the surface. Bowman and Maggot held the tether tight, the others took one last breath of oxygen, released their tanks and did a blow and go as they ascended to the surface, without rupturing their lungs on their ascent.

When they reached the surface, the men inflated the rest of the Zodiac and attached the 35 hp Evinrude motor to the back of the boat and hopped in. Wiz cranked up the motor as they all took their masks off. Hawk sat on the bow, Buck was in the middle and Wiz was at the controls.

As they motored towards shore, Wiz looked at the others, gave them a thumbs up, and they both returned the gesture, signaling they were good to go. Buck knew he was about to land at the gates of hell. There was no moon that night, and clouds had moved in and blanketed the night sky. The sea itself was rough and choppy.

"Looks like some bad weather's moving in," said Hawk.

"Yep," said Buck. "That can't be good."

"We're still sticking to the plan. We can't deviate now," said Wiz.

The Zodiac made its way stealthily over the waves. The boat was equipped with state-of-the-art technology that allowed it to evade detection by Iranian surface search radars. The boat also used radar-absorbing paint and was engineered with a combination of specially designed angles that allowed it to glide furtively through the water undetected.

The drop-off zone itself had been carefully selected. It was flanked by trees on one side, and a large quarry of rocks on the other. As the Zodiac approached, Buck readied himself. "You know the extraction plan, right?" Buck gave a thumb's up and rolled off the Zodiac into the sea. He had about a hundred yard swim to the shore.

When Buck made landfall, he slipped out of his wetsuit, put it in his waterproof rucksack and donned some casual clothes. Dressed in khaki shorts, a black t-shirt and thongs, Buck followed the shoreline near the small seaport village of Akhtar to the pre-planned drainage culvert that would lead him under the road and into the housing area where Agent Miller was residing. Clutching the rucksack in his hand as he crawled through the culvert, he could hear voices coming from the other end of the conduit where he needed to exit. He paused for several minutes, which seemed like an hour, then proceeded to the other side. As he hopped out of the drainage pipe a light rain began to fall. He quickly gathered his bearings, spotted his checkpoint, and proceeded to his destination. When he arrived at the apartment complex, he knocked on the door.

Knock. Knock Knock.

Agent Miller opened the door. "Gunny Cassidy, it's great to see you, Marine."

"Likewise, Agent. How's Iran treating you?"

"Oh, you know. Just dealing with the most deranged, powerful psychopath the world has ever known. Normal stuff."

Buck laughed. "Nothing a bullet to the skull can't cure, right?"

"I've already written out that prescription, believe it or not. Speaking of which, come over here and let me introduce you to my balcony."

The two men walked outside through the balcony doors. Agent Miller pointed towards the cafe. "Right there, Buck. That's where we'll be. See the table out in front, with the white lilies on it? The seat that faces the road, that's where the sonofabitch will be seated. My seat will be here," he said, pointing to the chair that faced the ocean. "And the dignitaries will be seated pretty much everywhere else. But, you should have a clean shot."

Buck nodded his head.

"And, I'm sure I don't have to remind you, you only

have one shot. Miss this, and you might not get a second chance. That being said, you know your shit. You'll hit him."

"Oh and, one last thing. I don't think anything will go wrong, but if it does, you'll see me move my wine glass from my right, to my left. When that happens, that means something has gone to shit."

"Understood. After I take the shot, you'll rendezvous back here, and then we'll make our way to the extraction point, correct?"

"Got it. Goddamn Savage. It's good to see you. We only have one more night. There's food in the fridge if you want it, but I'm hitting the sack. You need anything else from me?"

"No thanks, Bastos. I can take it from here."

"Alright, good night then."

"Good night."

With that, Bastos went to his room. Buck pulled a chair up to the balcony, and opened his duffle bag. The BLR Lightning Rifle was disassembled inside the bag. He pulled it out, and began attaching the pieces, staring directly at the seat where Tayyib Al'Qim would sit.

CHAPTER SEVENTEEN
BYE BYE BIRDIE

An Air Force C-17 was greeted by the morning sunrise as it taxied in front of a hangar at Roosevelt Roads, a United States Navy Base in Puerto Rico. Major Tim "Sidewinder" Lewis and his crew stepped off the back ramp of the C-17, and began to unload the contents of the plane.

"What's in the crates, Major?" the ramp crew asked.

"The crates," Lewis said, "hold wings and accessory parts for this state-of-the-art bird of prey."

"Has Christmas arrived early for someone?" they asked.

"You might say that," replied the Major.

The senior airman unhooked the drone from its pallet; the technical sergeant hooked a tow tractor up to it and towed it out of the cargo bay and into the hangar. Lewis' staff sergeant operated the forklift, which lifted the crates out of the plane and set them alongside the drone. The master sergeant watched over the men and assisted them while they assembled the drone's wings and attachments. When they finished, what they saw was a phenomenal piece of modern technology, the MQ-9 Reaper.

"This unmanned aerial vehicle (UAV) is a hunter-killer drone, designed for long endurance, long distance and high-altitude surveillance. What they don't tell you though, is that this robot packs a punch. The Reaper can carry fifteen times more ordnance than the MQ-1, and it's almost three times faster."

After several hours of assembling the drone, Major Lewis and his crew went for chow. After lunch, they checked all the Reaper's systems and then gave it a test fly.

During lunch the master sergeant asked his boss, "Well Major, who are we going to smoke this time?"

"I don't know master sergeant, it's on a need-to-know basis and I guess I don't have high enough clearance to be brought into the loop. Our mission is to get her ready, test fly it and wait for the order to launch and make the rendezvous with the satellite. Copy?"

"Roger". Now let's go test fly this baby."

December 7th, 2013
Time: 0700 AM

As Major "Herc" Valentine walked into the drone control room, he could tell that this would be no ordinary day. There were far too many generals standing around, even for a Reaper squadron. He was stopped before he could get to the operations desk.

"Major Valentine, you have a senior aircrew working with you today, and you'll be briefing over at the 107th Test Squadron," said the senior master sergeant. The Generals looked him over like he was a newbie. Herc signed off his currencies, and nodded his head. "I'm ready to go."

Herc and the generals arrived in the 107th after a short drive. Valentine sat his aircrew down in the weapons shop.

"Alright guys, wait here while I figure out what madness we have today," he said with a grin.

"Maybe we are here for a dog and pony show. Lots of generals around," said the twenty-three-year-old sensor operator, Vic.

"It better be quick. I have a dental exam at 1230," complained his mission coordinator, Fancy, a twenty-year-old from Texas. She checked her watch and leaned back in her chair.

Herc walked out to the operations floor and watched the aerial view of a single Reaper in flight, assigned the call sign Reaper 99. He couldn't tell where it was based on the coordinates. *Somewhere in bad guy land, safe to say,* he thought to himself. Herc felt a push on his shoulder. "Sit down, son," said the three-star general in a tight Army uniform. "You were selected for this mission by your commander. You have air-to-air expertise from your days in the F-16. Your record shows a TopGun award and a 100% hit rate with the long range missiles, and almost as good with the Aim-9. You think you can still shoot?"

Valentine grinned, knowing those promotion bullets are always inflated. "Don't tempt me. I can shoot, but the MQ-9 Reaper is an air-to-ground beast."

A two-star Air Force General sat down next to him with a dossier full of information. He flipped to a picture of an MQ-9, with two Aim-9X missiles on the wings. Herc tried to stifle a laugh but blurted out "That will never work." The General stood and commanded the aircrew to swing the ball aft, which showed the current ordnance of the lone flying MQ-9. The picture moved after a few moments and Herc couldn't believe his eyes: Two missiles. Aim-9X, right there on the rails.

Valentine walked to the screen showing the image. "Well, I'd love to be the guy that tests those for you. Where's this at? The Nevada range? Utah?"

"No, not quite. The North Atlantic," piped up the Army general. "And you have a mission to engage a high priority air-to-air target. We wanted the weapons officer to do it but he's TDY (temporary duty). You're next on our list. Congratulations." An intelligence officer handed him a smaller dossier of maps and rules. Herc began to scan through them, noticing that everyone in the room was staring at him.

"Well . . . I've never missed," he said.

An intelligence officer rolled her eyes and huffed, "Pilots."

Herc smiled back at her and thought, *I think we're both a little nervous.*

After perusing the documents, Herc walked back to his crew with the intelligence officer following directly behind. After Valentine briefed the crew on what he knew, he turned to the intelligence officer, "What the heck are we shooting? I see the ROE, (rules of engagement) the locations, and where I need to be at a precise time, but what's the target?"

"You don't need to know that, sir, you just need to call out the bearing and range of your target when your missile locks it, and we will verify the status of your target as hostile or non-player. You hear hostile and have the heat lock, then shoot both missiles. That's your mission."

Valentine looked at his crew. They were bewildered. Herc shook his head side to side. *No matter,* he thought to himself. *Just go back to basics: fly, fight, win.*

After the pep talk with himself, Herc walked back to the operations floor with his assistants. The radio chatter sped up and became increasingly purposeful. He told the supervisor he was ready to step. The supervisor looked over Herc's crew and gave the OK.

Valentine walked down the hall with quickened steps, followed by a procession of generals and officers. At the door to the GCS (ground control station), Herc looked at the eyes of his sensor who was noticeably distracted by the parade. "That's it, you can watch the show from the ops floor," Herc said. "My crew and I have a mission to fly. Please excuse us."

Major Valentine stepped into the GCS, flanked by the usual satellite and computer relays. He also had an additional laptop on the left side, in the pilot's seat. The current aircrew was glad to see them. "Dude, what'd you do, stop for coffee?" chirped the Pilot. "Get over here, and get in the seat. You have about an hour twenty until you are on the Vul (vulnerability)." Herc looked at the clock and noted the time.

The outgoing pilot pointed to the maps. "Here's the border, and here's the flight path of your target. You have about a three minute window or you'll lose your objective."

Major Valentine settled into his seat, adjusted the headset and lowered the chat screen so he could catch up on airspace and weather. The prior pilot and sensor grabbed their things and departed. Herc was left alone, with just his sensor in a room full of humming computers, and images of a rising sun.

Herc noticed that something was wrong right away. "Hey, my GPS appears accurate, but my location looks like it's blitzing all over the world. MC (mission coordinator), do you know anything about our Lat Long here? Do you see the coordinates jumping all over?"

The MC, at her own station on the operations floor yelled back, "Sir, there is nothing coming through here for me to see at all."

Then a voice came out over the intercom that surprised them all, "You will have no coordinates and you will not look down. We will guide you to the release point, and then we will direct you to engage. Do you understand?" Herc bolted back in his seat, unraveling, every fighter pilot nerve in his body inflamed with rage.

Whose mission is this? He thought.

His experienced sensor, Vic, lifted his mic away from his mouth and covered it so as not to be overheard. "Sir, this is Reaper, not Viper. You know the whole world is listening. I wouldn't be surprised if the president herself was watching this show," smiled Vic.

"You're right," Herc said off-mic, "let's just get this rollin."

Before he could finish, a secret chat room popped up on his screen. KING was the call sign (Command & Control at the Combined Air Operations Center). *Well, that must be the big boss himself,* Herc thought.

In a chat bubble, King typed, "Do a weapons and safety check; we're ahead of schedule. When you're armed hot and ready to engage, write me back."

Herc opened his weapons dialogue from the GCS computers as though it were a word document. He armed the weapons and waited for good tones on each. He tuned his radio to an air coordination frequency and heard a radio check from two aircraft.

"Jumper 11 check."

"Shaft 99, Jumper 11(fighter plane) is on station as fragged, goalie and get well skulling at your call."

Skulling, Major Valentine mused to himself, knowing that hardcore fighter pilots don't say head, or heading. "Good," he announced to Vic, "We've got fighters of some kind, probably F/A-18s."

The voice popped in across Herc's headset. "Sir, please do not speculate, and please keep all communications mission related at this time."

Herc opened his mouth to react, but he had received another chat from King. "Shaft, timeline slip left 15, control will be from Mother (C-41), please do your best to hit their timing."

Valentine wrote back, "King, Wilco."

On the ops floor, the MC (Fancy) had 12 screens opened up with charts, data, chat rooms, and intelligence feeds. She was dwarfed by the wall of data. She stood to read the first chat from Mother: "Shaft, proceed at maximum forward speed 277 degrees. Call out final speed, and maintain present altitude."

Fancy sat back down and pressed the hot mic button to talk. "Sir, did you see the chat from Mother?"

In the GCS, Herc throttled forward and headed west. "Mic, I got it. We're pouring all our fuel on the fire. Last ops check showed us fat on gas, but then again I don't really know where we are." He feigned a systems check and slid through a manual autopilot check, which was enough time to glance at the GPS data before it was obscured.

Hmmm. It looks normal for our usual AORs (area of responsibility), Herc breathed with a sigh of relief.

Vic piped up, "Now I know how a sub-driver feels. I can't see a thing."

Major Valentine nodded with little enthusiasm, as he was busy plotting their course on the blank map.

He frowned. *All our ground and location data is gone. Damn. Might as well give up on that and focus on target acquisition.*

"Scan west, Vic, full zoom."

Vic nodded and panned the Reaper's massive camera out front. He sharpened the image and picked up a tiny black dot above the horizon in infrared. The black dot meant that it was a hot target, and that it was flying. "Yep, we got something! But we don't have range information."

Alright, my speed is pegged and the temps are running hot. Yellow boxes . . . means that I'm pushing my engine too hard. And, looks like my missiles are greened up. Damn, this feels good. Got that good old fashioned air to air feeling like I'm in an F-16 even though I'm in a stationary room 4,000 miles away from my aircraft, Herc thought to himself.

Mother sent another chat: "Shaft, you're missing the window, you are authorized to exceed structural limitations."

King popped in: "Shaft 99, this is a CDE 5 High Target, Sec Def approved to engage once declared by Mother."

Mother: "You have OpCon."

"Copy that, Mother."

Herc stared at the black dot on the screen as it began to show a nose aspect. Vic zoomed in all the way and cranked up the digital refinement. He pointed out the thrust. Herc nodded, unsure of what he could say out loud.

He lifted his headset and covered it, "Vic, it looks like a turbojet, it's got some good trails on it."

"Yep. It's still too small to tell what it is."

Herc rubbed his eyes and turned the brightness up on the screen but he jumped when a warning buzzer blurted out with an annoying ring: "ENGINE TEMPERATURE—HIGH!"

Herc watched the trend on his instrument panel. He began to send a chat to Mother, but before he could finish, the mysterious voice rang out over his headset, "Shaft 99 you are cleared to engage target, bearing 275, range 42 miles, forty-three thousand feet. Hostile."

Before he could respond, Mother typed in a nearly identical message: "Shaft 99, Mother, target is declared hostile. Stand by for clearance to fire."

Herc responded instinctively. "Commit Commit Commit."

We're in, and we're nearly on fire, he thought to himself.

He lifted the MASTER ARM switch. *I don't know why I always do that. I have to do it on the computer screen. Ah, oh well. I'll do both just in case.*

Vic refined his picture, and Herc started to make out two distinct engines on a larger aircraft. Over his headset he heard, "Shaft 99, you are in the WEZ(weapons employment zone), you are in the WEZ, you are in the WEZ."

Herc looked at Vic, who nodded, that's the best picture he can get. Major Valentine placed his hand on the missile trigger, and squeezed one detent. LEFT WEAPON—READY.

Herc sent a chat to King, "I'm unable to determine correlation to your declaration of hostile, can you confirm via off board sources before I shoot."

King sent back in all capital letters, "SHOOT!"

A second later, Jumper 11 barked over the radio "Shaft 99, Jumper 11: the airspace is clear for over 110 miles around your target, so if you see something in the air, to your west, that is your target. We're above you at angels 510 block 550 and have a clear picture to your west. You have a good Dec from Mother."

Herc uncaged the Aim-9X and listened for a good tone. It settled on an average tone. "Hmm," he mused to himself. "Distance must be a problem. Without gauges, I have no idea how far away I am from the target. Or even what the target is!"

Herc watched the image for a second more, trying to get as close as possible. He squeezed just as he heard "You are out of the WEZ."

He responded with "Shaft 99, Fox 2." He heard a sharp tone on the second missile. "Alright, I'm in the zone now." He squeezed off the second missile. "Shaft 99, Fox 2, winchester."

Herc pulled the power back and . . . there was silence, nothing. Everything was eerily quiet. He tended to his burning hot engine and climbed in idle to cool off and slow down.

On the screen, he could see two streaks heading toward

the single spot, the black dot on the screen. Suddenly, he saw an impact, and a streak, like a black and white image of a meteor flashing and pulsing. There was a second flash. Both missiles had impacted, and the aircraft spiraled down to the ocean shattered in pieces.

"Shaft, Kill, single hostile, west."

Jumper 11 chimed in, "Shaft, Mother, we confirm the splash, target is off radar. Radar is clear at 110."

A chat from Mother popped up: "Turn east and RTB. Nice show."

King chatted in: "Sierra Hotel!"

A knock was heard at the GCS door. Herc turned to see the Air Force general. He walked in and patted him on the back.

"Could you hear the tone? Is that why you fired again after the WEZ had closed?" Herc suddenly realized that he had a sick bird and turned back to the instrument panels, scrolling through Emergency Procedure pages.

"Yes sir. Lock, Dec, Shoot. I heard a weak growler on one, so I shot again."

"Good," beamed the General.

"By the way," Herc asked, "What did we shoot?"

The General smiled and patted him on the back again.

"Two missiles. That's all you need to know."

CHAPTER EIGHTEEN
ROLLING THUNDER

December 7th
Sweetwater and BigHands
Time: 1500

"Alright rookie, are you ready? This is the big show," Sweetwater said.

"Yes, sir, as ready as I'll ever be," BigHands replied.

After an intensive briefing, the two pilots sat waiting to man-up for their launch in the Gunslinger's ready room. Today was game day, and you could feel the tension on the ship. CAG took a look at Johnson. He could see that the lad was nervous and stressed. After the incident in Hawaii, and being stuck on the ship for most of the trip, Sweetwater understood his emotions. "Look, Son, before we launch, I want to talk to you about something."

"Of course, sir. What is it?"

"I want to talk to you about Hawaii."

Matt saw Johnson's face droop. "I know sir. And I'm sorry; I promise it won't happen again."

CAG put his hand on Johnson's shoulder. "Listen, I was your age once too. Believe me, I know how it is. When you get too much whiskey in you, and light your hair on fire, anything can go wrong. But, that doesn't excuse us from our duties. You were the senior officer in your group and you should have provided better leadership. You should not have engaged in foolishness mooning citizens in a pool."

Johnson's heart sank. "Yes, sir."

"I know that Skipper Petriccione has already tongue-lashed you. And he had to—hell, I have to! Like I said though, we know how it is, we've been there. But, I see something in you, Gary. In more ways than I can count. I see a lot of me in you. Or at least, me when I was younger. You've got that fire, that ambition. I can see it in your eyes."

Johnson's eyes began to light up. Matt continued, "All we have to do is harness that energy and that passion. And that is exactly why I chose you to be my wingman for this flight. I had the chance to dismiss you from this mission after the Hawaii tomfoolery, but I didn't, because I still believe in you. Hell, we all believe in you. The question is, do you believe in yourself?"

Johnson looked at CAG. "Yes, sir."

"I'm sorry son, I didn't hear you."

"Yes, sir." Johnson said, with more enthusiasm.

"Louder, sailor!" Sweetwater said.

"Hell fuckin' yes, sir!" said Johnson at the top of his lungs.

Matt laughed. "Now that is what I'm talking about! C'mon BigHands, let's go move some dirt."

The two men went to their gear lockers and suited-up, then made their way to flight deck control. The pilots'

F-35C *Lightnings* were fueled, loaded with their weapons and parked on the fantail. Before they separated to do their individual pre-flights, CAG said, "Alright, stay on my wing. You know what to do, let's kick the tires and light the fires".

The two men strapped into their planes, and made their way to catapults one and three. While sitting on the cats, Sweetwater came voiced over tactical radio and asked BigHands if he was ready to rock and roll. A double click came back over the radio to CAG.

Agent Miller and Buck Cassidy
Time: 1715

"Looks like your friends are starting to gather at the café," Buck said to Bastos, peering through his rifle's scope. "Looks like there's about eight in total, including our target."

"That's the full group, then. Those dignitaries you see are from Egypt, Iraq, Saudi Arabia, Syria, Yemen, Libya, and Kuwait. If those countries shift, the remaining Arab nations will collapse, just like dominos," Agent Miller replied.

"That's why we're here, then. So to clarify, the target is only Tayyib Al'Qim? Not the other dignitaries?" Savage asked.

"Not if we can help it, no. With Tayyib dead, the entire plan falls apart. We don't want any collateral damage."

"Understood."

Bastos picked up his briefcase. "Okay so, let's go over this one more time. I'm going to go down there and talk up Al'Qim's plan. We keep them there until the CHAMP missile from the Gunslingers goes off. That's the EMP (Electro-Magnetic-Pulse, so this entire area will start to go dark. When those lights are out, take your shot. In the confusion that follows, we'll meet back here, then we'll head back through the drainage pipe out into the gulf for our pick-up."

"Easy enough. And if there are any problems, you'll put your wine glass to your left."

"Exactly. Hopefully that won't happen, though." Agent Miller walked over to the front door. "Good luck, Savage." Miller opened the door. "Oh, and one more thing, Buck."

"Yeah?"

"Don't fuckin' shoot me."

Buck laughed. "Stay safe, check your six."

With that, Bastos walked out the front door.

The night air felt cool on his skin. A light mist of rain was blanketing the city, and you could hear the rumble of thunder off in the distance. In spite of the dampness the city was alive with people coming and going, eating, talking, and enjoying their lives. Agent Miller made his way through the small village until he reached the cafe. He noticed Tayyib Al'Qim and the seven other dignitaries sitting in their seats, seemingly waiting for him.

"Ah, there he is!" Al'Qim said, standing up. "The man of the hour, the man we have been waiting for! As salamu alaykum."

"As salamu alaykum to you as well. I apologize for being late." Bastos said as he sat down in his seat. He noticed the other dignitaries were shifting nervously, and that there were several other members in the cafe staring

139

intently at him. "Is . . . everything alright?"

Tayyib Al'Qim smiled. "Oh yes, yes! We've just been anxiously awaiting your arrival . . . Agent Craig Miller."

Sweetwater and BigHands
Time: 1730

The catapult officers on cat one and three put CAG and BigHands' aircraft into tension. Both bow and waist catapult officers raised one of their legs and shook it in the air for a second, then placed it back on the deck, while they waited for the salute back from the pilots, indicating they were ready to be launched. As BigHands checked his controls and instruments, he thought to himself, *What the hell was that leg shake all about?* Still a fledging carrier aviator, he'd soon find out. He quickly got his mind back in the ball game and made his salute to the catapult officer. When the second hand on the catapult officers' watches hit 30, they knelt down, touched the deck with their extended arm, signing to fire the cats.

As the two aircraft hurled down the cat-tracks, BigHands realized this was no ordinary cat-shot. It caged his eyeballs and grayed him out three quarters of the way down the catapult. Once off the cat, he shook his head, cleared the cobwebs away and started to join up on CAG's aircraft. *Holy shit!* he thought, *What the hell just happened?*

Being a smart young man with an engineering degree from the Naval Academy, he soon figured out what the leg shake meant. Due to his aircraft's weight, he needed a heavier shoot to ensure a safe end-speed. He knew he was heavy, because he'd signed his weight sheet when he put it in the box in flight deck control. However, he forgot about the consequential jolt the heavier catapult shot produced.

The weather was getting worse as dash-two began to rendezvous on CAG's plane. As BigHands closed the gap and started to tuck-up under CAG's left wing, he felt something rubbing against the bottom of his right wrist. He took a quick peek down by his stick hand and could see a panel that had started to come loose. He jiggled it around a bit, but then continued to fly the aircraft and joined up with CAG.

CAG looked at BigHands when he was aboard, gave a thumbs up, asking him with a hand signal if he was okay. BigHands returned the signal. The less chatter on the radio the better, just in case someone on the receiving end of their payload picked up on their frequency.

The two Gunslingers were flying at five hundred feet off the deck headed towards the Bushehr Nuclear Power Plant. There was no turning back now. As they started to hit their turning point for their bombing run, BigHands was distracted by the loose panel again. After fumbling with it a second time, to no avail, Johnson slipped behind CAG's plane and climbed to two thousand feet.

Agent Miller
Time: 1758

"I'm sorry, I'm afraid I don't know what you mean," Bastos stammered out. His heart had stopped.

"Cut the bullshit, Miller. I know all about you. Your

little charade is over."

Agent Miller gritted his teeth. "Sorry to disappoint, Mr. Al'Qim. However, you said you wanted deception." Bastos leaned back in his chair. "So, I gave you deception."

Al'Qim smirked. "Oh yes, yes you did. Quite impressive, in fact. So impressive, that you might have actually gotten away with it, but your government ratted you out."

Agent Miller didn't let his eyes betray him, but he was shocked. *Betrayed me? How?* He cleared his throat before he said, "Betrayed me? I think you got your facts wrong."

"Oh, I think not," Al'Qim said as he took a folder from his briefcase and handed it to Bastos. "A few hours ago, a very special plane involved with this operation was shot down. A plane very near and dear to my heart." Al'Qim waved two fingers at Bastos, and out of the corner of his eye, Agent Miller could see three men seated throughout the cafe brandishing automatic weapons.

"At first," Al'Qim continued, "I didn't think anything of it. I knew the CIA would dig into this, and I knew that eventually, it would be shot down. However, then I began to think about the timing of it all. How suspicious that this would happen on the very day I was planning on putting my plan into motion?"

"Some might say providence," Bastos said with a smirk.

"Ah, yes. Some might say that. Some, however, might say *a rat*. The events lined up perfectly. So, I did a little more digging on the people who had recently come into my life. So then, I did a little digging on my protégé, you. Turns out you actually are quite fond of America, aren't you? Fond enough to work for the CIA, anyway."

"I'm also not a big fan of soccer, either, so there's at least a couple things I lied to you about." Agent Miller said as he moved his wine glass to his left.

Al'Qim chuckled. "Oh yes, continue with the jokes. You'll soon realize that there is nothing funny about the men that break my trust." With that, he waved two fingers again at Bastos. The three armed men stood up.

"So, I have decided to make your death the beginning of my victory, and these dignitaries will watch what we do to Americans who forget their place in this new world. Any last words, Agent Miller?"

Buck Cassidy
Time: 1759

"Shit. He moved the wine glass to his left," Buck said to himself aloud, as he peered through the scope. "Sonofabitch," he said again, as he saw the three men armed with Uzi's stand up. They began to advance towards Agent Miller with their guns drawn. The crowd in the cafe seemed oblivious to the situation developing.

Think, dammit, think! If I shoot Al'Qim now, they'll shoot Bastos. If I shoot the guys on Bastos, Al'Qim will run away. I need that EMP. Damn it, Sweetwater, we need you!"

Sweetwater and BigHands
Time: 1800

Alright, *ten miles to target. Time to prime these missiles up. BigHands began* climbing to two thousand feet. As he was doing that, he dropped his right hand off the stick and flipped the arming switch on for the CHAMP missiles.

Nothing happened.

What the fuck? He thought as he moved the switch back and forth several times. *Where's the arming light?*

"Sonofabitch," he said aloud. "What the fuck is wrong?" He quickly broke radio silence, "CAG, I've got a problem . . . I can't arm the missiles."

"What's the matter?"

"Not sure, I need to make a couple racetrack circles and troubleshoot."

"Make it quick, I'll slow down and circle below you."

BigHands' mind was racing a mile a minute. *The panel, the panel, it has to do with that panel.* Suddenly BigHands figured it out. *Aha! It must have been the Cat shot . . . something must have come loose.*

He lifted one side of the panel and put his hand under it; he could feel a bundle of wire. He started to wiggle it back and forth and his arming light started to flicker. *Shit,* he thought. When they wired his plane for the CHAMPS at Kirkland Air Force Base, something must have come loose. That plane had made over 150 carrier landings and cat shots, since they'd left on cruise; it was possible one of the wires worked itself loose.

BigHands radioed, "CAG! I've found the problem; the wiring to my trigger is FUBAR."

"Work the problem; we've got to start our run-in now." Sweetwater transmitted.

"Roger", replied BigHands.

BigHands was on the backside of his turn at two

thousand feet and CAG was in trail about a quarter of a mile at five hundred feet. BigHands began to really shake the bundle of wire at this point and he got a steady light, off and on for a few seconds. At that point, he knew where the problem was located. *"Found it, you sonofabitch.*

As he started to roll out on his five mile run-in line, he called CAG and told him to slow up to 250 knots. BigHands checked his line-up, put the F-35C *Lightning* on autopilot and grabbed his survival knife. He yanked it out of his vest, reached over to the panel, ripped open the back-side corner and spotted the zip-tie that was holding the bundle of wires together. With his knife, he cut the zip-tie and freed up the wires.

At that instant, Matt called BigHands, "I'm stepping up my speed for my weapons delivery."

"Let her rip CAG, I'm about to turn out the lights."

"Roger," CAG replied.

BigHands could clearly see the lights from the city and the power plant, now. When he got to his firing point, he pulled the trigger . . . but nothing happened. *You Motherfucker, come on!*

The arming light withstood his verbal abuse. With the trigger squeezed, he frantically moved the wires back and forth. Suddenly, both CHAMP missiles fired and left the rails. BigHands yanked his plane to the left and started climbing to twenty thousand feet. As he looked over his shoulder, he saw the two missiles streak over the city. He started to sing, "Turn out the lights the party's over!" but abruptly stopped, when he saw his cockpit begin to fill with smoke.

**Agent Miller
Time: 18:02**

For Bastos, time stood still. As he watched his life flash before his eyes, there was only one thing he could focus on, *he failed.* He watched the armed men turn off their safeties, and aim their weapons at him.

"Don't make me ask again, Agent Miller. I'm doing you a courtesy, for what reason I'm not quite sure, let's call it a professional courtesy. We used to be colleagues, anyway. So, answer me. Do you have any last words?"

"Last words? Other than 'fuck you', I think I'm fresh out of last words."

"Ah well. Arrogant as ever. I gave you your chance." Al'Qim looked at the three armed men. "Shoot him."

Out of the corner of his eye, Agent Miller saw a fast streak of light race over the night sky. *A shooting star? Hmphh. I wish . . . I was anywhere but here.*

**Buck Cassidy
Time: 1803**

"Time to make a decision, Buck. Bastos would want you to take the shot, to kill Al'Qim. He knew the risks, he knew that this was a possibility. You can't let down the entire world just to save a fellow soldier."

Cassidy sighed, peering down the scope of his rifle. The crosshairs were lasered on the skull of Tayyib Al'Qim, who had a smirk on his face as he talked to Bastos.

"Damn. Bastos. I know you can't hear me, but I'm sorry man. I know this means that you might die, but we'll have killed the biggest threat to the world since Adolf Hitler. I'm so very sorry."

Buck Cassidy took a deep breath, placed his finger on the trigger of his BLR Lightning rifle, and squeezed the trigger.

The lights went out.

Sweetwater and BigHands
Time: 18:04

Nice *job kid,* Matt thought to himself as the CHAMP missiles went off, emitting electromagnetic pulses that cut power to the city. Now that the "Fat Lady was Singing", Sweetwater started his climb to fifteen hundred feet, not knowing the trouble BigHands was having in his cockpit. Still undetected, he opened his bomb-bay doors, flipped the arming switch to arm, and said to himself, "Here come the fireworks!" With that, he released his payload.

Agent Miller
Time: 18:05

Bastos *thought to himself, as the lights went out, this works too!* There was a rumble throughout the crowd, and some were beginning to panic. Tayyib Al'Qim rose nervously from his seat. "What is this? What's happeni—" SPLAT. Buck's bullet pierced Tayyib's skull, dropping him dead.

Instantly Agent Miller reached under the table and grabbed the hidden 9 millimeter pistol that was taped there for emergencies just like this one. He pulled it out, aimed at one of the armed guards, and squeezed off three rounds. The bullets riddled the man's chest, and he collapsed.

In the darkness and confusion, Bastos quickly turned towards the second guard whose Uzi was aimed at him. Agent Miller kicked a chair, flinging it towards the guard and buckling his knees. Bastos quickly fired two bullets searing the guard's brain.

Alright, just one guard left, he thought, Bastos felt a sharp, tearing pain rip through his right shoulder. "Ah fuck!" he said, causing him to drop his pistol. He turned to his right and saw the last guard approaching him, about to finish the job.

At that moment, a huge, earth-shattering explosion rocked the city of Bushehr. The explosion caused the guard to miss his aim. Bastos groped for his pistol, and then heard the sound of a body falling to the ground. The last guard was dead, courtesy of a bullet to the skull from Buck Cassidy.

Agent Miller laid there for a moment, and took a deep breath as the rain fell on his face. "Holy shit. That was the best shooting star I've ever seen."

Sweetwater and BigHands
Time: 1807

Within twenty seconds of releasing his payload, Sweetwater watched as a destructive swath of 1000 pound bombs left a grave of fifty yards wide and three hundred yards long. At the end of his bombing run, he closed the bomb-bay doors and made a seven (g) pull-up into a half Cuban eight and started heading back to the ship, looking for BigHands.

Johnson was assholes and elbows trying to clear the smoke from the cockpit. He knew the smoke wasn't from the engine bleed or ECS duct, because of its white color.

CAG came up on the radio, "Dash-two this is Gunslinger, what's your posit?"

"I'm at twenty thousand feet heading 270, 50 miles from mother (Carrier). I've got smoke in the cockpit."

"Do you have an open fire?"

"Negative, I believe it's an electrical short from that wire bundle."

"Fly the plane, do your emergency procedure for smoke in the cockpit and I'll rendezvous on you."

"Roger."

"Put your wing lights to flash."

"Copy."

BigHands put his pressure switch to RAM/Dump, then he turned his cabin temperature knob to full counterclockwise and slowed to two hundred knots. The smoke started to dissipate from the cockpit. When he looked out, CAG was off his Starboard wing.

"How we doing BigHands?"

"I've got it under control now."

"Great I've got the lead and I'll take us home."

"Roger that," BigHands replied.

"Hell of a job son, I don't know what you had to do, but you got-r-done."

"It wasn't pretty," Johnson replied.

"We'll debrief once we're on the deck. By the way, when I checked in, they said the deck was moving around, be ready to fly a varsity pass."

"Roger that sir."

Buck Cassidy
Time: 1810

Buck quickly grabbed the waterproof rucksack with their gear and ran out of the apartment into the street. He met up with Bastos in a nearby alleyway.

"What the fuck are you doing here?" Bastos breathed. "The rendezvous was at the apartment!"

"You got shot, that's what happened! C'mon, I've already gathered your gear. Let's get out of here. How's your wound?"

"Ah, it's a flesh wound, it hurts like hell, but believe me, I've had worse."

The pandemonium in the streets provided substantial cover as the two men entered the drainage pipe which led out to the beach.

"So what happened?" Buck asked.

"The bastards found me out and linked me to shooting of Flight IA 0000."

"Sonofabitch."

"Yeah. You're telling me."

"What about the dignitaries?"

"Well, he was using me as an example for them, I think. He wanted to show them how he would deal with people that didn't agree with him. Didn't work out so well for him, did it? After the shot, most of them scattered. And now with the destruction of the nuclear power plant, I think they realized the error of their ways."

"I think you're likely right."

As the two men exited the drainage pipe, the storm was raging even harder.

"I can't fuckin' see anything! Gonna have to light my flare!" Buck said, as he reached into his bag and grabbed his pencil flare. He aimed it toward the sky and fired.

"Hope they saw that."

A few minutes later, the two men saw the Zodiac, and two familiar faces.

"Looks like you boys need a ride," Wiz said, as they pulled up.

"Oh shit! Are you hit?" Wiz asked, noticing Bastos shoulder wound.

"Yeah, but it's not a big deal. Just a flesh wound."

"We'll get you patched up once aboard the sub", Hawk said.

Wiz navigated the Zodiac back to where the sub was submerged. The men then worked their way in reverse; they deflated the Zodiac, and began to swim down towards the Shed. They tethered everything onto the sled, and then slipped inside the DDS itself. When they were all inside, Commander Bowman flushed and pressurized the SHED. Once dry, they opened the hatch and entered the sub.

"Sonofabitch," Bastos said, it's great to be back on U.S. soil."

CHAPTER NINETEEN

"E" TICKET RIDE

Sweetwater and BigHands
Time: 1842

The weather was continually getting worse as CAG and BigHands made their way back to the USS Reagan. As the Gunslinger flight got closer to the ship, CAG checked in with Strike. "Strike, Gunslinger 201 on your 180 radial at angles 15, Squawking 6563, 5.1."

"Roger, Gunslinger 201. Squawk 5186, Altimeter 2984. Switch to Marshall," was the response from the *Reagan's* controller.

"Roger, switching."

"Marshall, this is Gunslinger 201 on your 180 radial at angles 15, squawking 5186, 5.1 Altimeter 2984".

Marshall replied, "Roger 201. BRC (basic recovery course) is 300. Marshall on the 120 radial, angels five, twenty miles. Expected recovery time 55. Time in ten seconds 1845." BigHands aircraft was 203, he was at angels sixteen at twenty-one miles and his push time was 56.

The deck was pitching ten to twenty feet, Cmdr. Sandy Mapleford (S+9), the CAG LSO, (landing signal officer) would do the waving tonight. He was the best paddles in the Navy. If the seas were angry, his calming voice was the one you wanted to hear as you came down the chute. Due to the heavy seas, the Fresnel lens was out of limits; therefore, (S + 9) would be working the Movlas (Manually Operated Visual Landing Aid) tonight.

Sweetwater was on his last lap in the holding pattern. As he began his descent, he contacted the ship. "201 commencing. 2984. 5.0." Approaching the ten-mile point, the ship's controller told him, "Go dirty and slow to approach speed." Sweetwater lowered his landing gear, flaps and hook. He also reduced his speed to 128 knots. Matt was still flying with the aid of his instruments until he got a quarter mile from the ship.

When he reached a quarter mile, the controller said, "201 call the ball". Sweetwater made the call. "201, Lightning Ball, 4.5" At this point CAG switched his attention from his instrument panel to the "MEATBALL" a quarter of a mile away on the portside of the flight deck.

S+9 piped up. "Good evening, CAG, ships moving a bit tonight, we're on the Movlas."

"Roger Movlas," CAG replied.

"Don't climb, the deck is down," replied Sandy.

As Matt got within a few hundred feet of the rounddown (back of the ship) the Meatball was all over the lens. Off the top, off the bottom, CAG didn't feel comfortable and started to add go-around thrust just as S+9 said, "Wave-off! Wave-off! Wave-off, 201, Wave it off!"

Sweetwater poured the coal to his aircraft as the deck fell out from underneath him and rolled about five degrees to the right. *Holy Shit,* Sweetwater thought to himself, *I goddamn near bought the farm on that pass*. He leveled his wings and climbed back to fifteen hundred feet. Mapleford came up on the blower; "Good job, CAG, the ship took an ugly roll as you came over the ramp. We'll get you aboard on the next pass."

"Roger," GAG replied.

By this time, BigHands was a quarter of a mile behind the ship. His ass was so tight you couldn't drive a knitting needle through it with a sledge hammer. As he called the ball, Sandy said, watch your line-up, "you're drifting starboard". BigHands made a slight correction and kept her coming. As he crossed the ramp, he could hear Mapleford saying, "line-up, line-up!" He dipped his left wing to correct his position and then his plane slammed onto the deck. The tailhook skipped the one wire and crabbed the two as he came to a violent stop.

As he raised his hook and taxied to the bow, he thought to himself, *I think I besmirched my flight suit*.

At that point the Air Boss, Commander, Beresky, came-up on tactical: "Nice job, BigHands, welcome to carrier aviation."

With the ship pitching and rolling, BigHands got vertigo so bad he had to stop taxiing for a moment. Once he was clear of the landing area and over the safe launch-line, he motioned to the Yellow-Shirt to chock and chain him, right where he'd stopped. After he shut the aircraft down and got out of the plane, he told his Yellow-shirt, that he didn't have the balls to taxi any further.

"No problem," said the Yellow-shirt. "It's mighty nasty out here".

BigHands said, "No shit", as he headed to flight deck control.

As Sweetwater lined up for his second pass, it looked like all of the carrier's four props were out of the water. *Goddamn!* he thought to himself, as he continued his approach.

Sandy was talking to him more than normal, due to the ships movement. "CAG, you're looking good, keep her coming. The deck's up, don't chase the ball, easy, easy with it, keep her coming, you're looking good."

Matt thought to himself. *I haven't seen the ship move like this in years.*

As Sweetwater crossed the ramp, the ship started to fall out from under him again. Sandy said in a stern voice, "Power, power, power!" Sweetwater jammed the throttle to the detent as his *Lightning* SLAMMED on the deck. His tailhook bounced over the number one and two wires and snagged the number three wire.

Holy Fuck, Matt said to himself as the aircraft started to decelerate. *Whew! Close one,.* Matt thought. His heart froze in place as he felt the sudden release from deceleration. The next thing he heard was the Air Boss and LSO, simultaneously yelling over the radio, "EJECT! EJECT! EJECT!" The number three arresting wire broke and his plane was skidding towards the port catwalk.

"*Sonofabitch*, I'm outta here!" he said, as he pulled the ejection handle between his legs. The canopy blew off and his rocket seat propelled him a hundred plus feet into the air. With the man-seat-separation and the deployment of his chute, CAG watched his aircraft tumble into "Davy Jones' Locker" below and then CAG was swallowed up by the sea. Capt. Morley ordered the ship to come to a heading of 260 and all engines back two-thirds.

The ship went to General Quarters, the flight deck crew ran to the portside of the ship and broke open their Chem-Light-Sticks and threw them into the water to mark where CAG went in. The Air Boss directed the SAR helo that was in starboard delta to head to the portside of the ship.

Lt. Cmdr. Nicky Mather was the aircraft commander flying the SAR mission that night. From the starboard side of the carrier, she bustered to the portside and started her search and rescue pattern.

S+9 spotted CAG, as he floated by the ship. Being an experienced LSO, he'd been in this situation before and had an eye for what a downed piloted looked like floating on the surface. It appeared that Matt's salt-water squibs had activated and disconnected him from his chute after water entry. His float-collar had inflated and Mapleford was able to see the reflection tape on his helmet, which caught his eye.

Once Sandy had his eye on the downed pilot, he never took his eyes off him. He grabbed the mic from one of his training LSO's and directed "Siren" above CAG. Lt. Cmdr. Mather had pulled several pilots out of the drink before and she knew the drill.

She positioned the helo upwind of CAG, put the SAR swimmer in the water, he then swam up to Sweetwater. By this time the hoist operator had lowered the horse–collar in the water. Siren backed her helo up, so as to drag the collar beside the swimmer. He reached out, grabbed the collar and attached it around and under Matt's armpits.

Then he wrapped himself around CAG's torso and legs. With that complete, he gave the hoist operator a thumbs-up as he reeled in the cable and lifted both of them out of the water and into the helo safely. As the swimmer laid CAG down on the floor of the helicopter, Nicky asked, "How is he?"

"Not good," was the response. "He's not breathing," the swimmer said alarmingly. "He's not breathing"

CHAPTER TWENTY

BOOMERANG

Matt opened his eyes and was greeted by a bright light. "Where . . . where am I?" he asked, unsure if he was asking it to anyone. "Am I dead?"

"No, Capt. Sullivan, you are not dead. You're in sick-bay." a man in a white doctor's coat answered.

"Sick-bay?"

"Yes sir! You're alive and well! Banged up a bit, but you're well. Remember me? I'm the Combat Quack! Your flight surgeon!"

"Doc Randolph."

"Yes, sir, that's me!"

"Thanks for stitching me up, doc. How bad was it?"

"Well, your aircraft ejection was pretty violent, so we've had to keep you sedated for a few days to stabilize your vital signs."

"What about the mission, and Johnson?" CAG asked.

"Everything worked as planned. We're waiting to see what the effects are going to be. There were a few mistakes on the ground, but as for you and BigHands, you ripped that nuclear plant a new asshole.

Shit hot, Matt thought to himself.

"Johnson's safe and sound. He's been down to check on you several times, in fact."

"He's a good man", Matt replied.

Matt pushed himself up on the back of the bed. "So, when can I get back to work Doc?"

"Not so fast," Doc Randolph said. "We're going to medevac you back to the states tomorrow."

"What? You can't do that! Why?"

"You're going home early! Your job is completed here."

"Bullshit. I've got another two months on deployment!"

"Listen CAG; unless you want to go home in a body-bag, you listen to me. There are many more tests that need to be done and we don't have the equipment on the ship to perform them. Therefore, tomorrow, we're flying you off the ship on the COD and a C-17 will fly you from Dubai back to San Diego. That's an order, Captain."

Sweetwater sighed. The look in Randolph's eyes told him that there was no convincing him otherwise. "Got it, Doc."

The Medevac flight to the states was a long and uneventful journey, even with the overnight in Hawaii. Matt's final leg from Hawaii to the mainland was much more enjoyable for him because, the Aircraft Commander, Captain Adam Moiles invited him up to the flight deck and allowed him to sit at the controls, which made the six hour flight go by faster for him.

The C-17 landed at the Naval Air Station North Island around two in the afternoon. Shortly after landing, Matt was taken to the Balboa Naval Hospital. Once there, his case was reviewed by the Chief-of-Staff and his orthopedic surgeons. They took X-Rays, ran some tests and then released him after three and a half hours of observation and examinations.

As Matt was about to leave Balboa, the head of orthopedic surgery stopped him.

"Captain, while we were examining you, you mentioned some neck and back pain."

"Yes Sir?"

"Well, pain like that is not uncommon after the trauma you experienced. I recommend that you go see Dr. Julie LaBarge."

"Julie LaBarge?"

"Yes, Captain, she's one of the best Chiropractors on the West Coast, and she's been cleared by the Navy's Bureau of Medicine to treat military personnel. She'll be able to relieve that back and neck pain for you."

"Thanks doc, I will! I'll give her a call."

Matt's first night back at home was a rough one. The house was lonely and dark, and Boomer's absence made it much worse for him. He decided to rest easy for the next few days. He did have one plan; he was going to call Mary. He wanted to see her badly, but a nagging pain in his ear was keeping him up most of the night.

"What if this is serious? I should probably get this checked out before I get in touch with Mary," he thought to himself.

On the third day of next to no sleep, he decided to go see his family physician, Dr. Eva Abbo. She had been his doctor for over twenty years. As he sat in the waiting room, Sweetwater could tell that he was being stared at by her receptionist, Karen. Matt chuckled to himself.

I still looked pretty banged up from the plane ejection, he thought. *Must be a sight for sore eyes.*

Brynne, her nurse, called Matt to their lab to draw blood and to check his vitals. As he was finishing up, Dr. Eva walked by and shockingly said, "My God, Matt! What happened to you?"

"Well . . ." he began.

"Not here. Please come into my office."

After a half hour of explaining the accident and all the idle chit chat Dr. Eva asked, "What can I do for you Matt?"

"Well, Doc, I've had an ear ache for the last several days and I can't seem to get rid of it."

"Let me take a look," replied Eva.

Taking her otoscope, she inspected his ear. After a few minutes, she said, "Your eardrum appears to be swollen and inflamed, are you experiencing any vertigo? Hearing loss?"

"No, ma'am," Matt replied.

"Your eardrum does not appear ruptured, so I'm going to give you some ear drops and antibiotics. This will kill the bacteria causing the ear infection and the drops will help the swelling and pain."

"Thank you, Dr. Eva," Matt said as he got up to leave.

"Wait a second, Matt; while you're here I want to check you over. Please remove your shirt and lie down on the examining table."

"You got it, Doc." Sweetwater took off his shirt and lay on his back as requested. Dr. Eva took her stethoscope, the common medical acoustic tool used to listen to the heart, lungs, abdomen and pulses in the neck. After several passes over Matt's chest and abdomen, she asked him

161

to stand and listened even more intently. He complied.

Matt watched her examine his chest, and he could see a concerned look on her face, which began to worry him.

"Everything okay, doc?"

She abruptly took the stethoscope off his chest and said, "Matt, I don't like what I'm hearing here. I'm going to call Dr. Rubenson, a cardiologist at Scripps Green Hospital and I want you to see him tomorrow."

"What's the problem Dr. Eva?"

"It may be nothing, Matt, I thought I heard some irregularities with your heart beat and I want Rubenson to give you a more thorough check. He's the best in the business."

Matt's heart sunk. "O-okay Doctor, what do I need to do?"

"Just put drops in your ear twice a day, take one pill a day and I'll see you back here in a week. I'll have Doctor Rubenson's office call you this afternoon to set up the appointment."

"Okay," Matt replied, his mind swirling with questions.

As he opened the door to leave, Dr. Eva smiled and said, "Take care of yourself, Matt, I'll see you in a week."

Still in a daze, Matt left her office and drove home, his anxiety level rising by the second. Once he arrived, he put the drops in his ear, took the prescribed medication and laid down for a short nap. It was interrupted an hour later by a phone call. It was Dr. Rubenson's assistant, Lisa."

"Good Afternoon, may I speak to Captain Sullivan?"

"This is he," Matt replied.

"Hi, my name is Lisa—I work for Dr. Rubenson. He'd

like to see you tomorrow morning at Scripps Green Hospital in La Jolla at nine o'clock. Can you have someone drive you to and from the hospital?"

"Yes, yeah sure, I should be able to find someone. What for?"

"He's going to do a procedure called a Transesophageal Echocardiogram to get high-quality moving pictures of your heart and you'll be sedated for the procedure. Therefore, you'll need someone to drive you."

"Understood. I can do that."

"Please fast twelve hours before you arrive, wear comfortable clothes, sweat pants and long sleeve shirt is preferred. Go to the third floor waiting room and his nurse Jessica will assist you. Any questions?"

"I don't think so. Thank you."

"We'll see you tomorrow, Captain Sullivan."

Holy shit, Matt thought to himself as he hung up the phone.

After several minutes of gathering his thoughts, Matt started wondering who could drive him. When he heard Scripps Green, he immediately thought of Dr. Mary Farrio.

She works there! But . . . I haven't seen or talked to her since Dubai. And, I don't know what's up with my health . . . maybe it's best to hold off on that. Matt wracked his brain, trying to think of anyone else. *Wait a minute! The Flintom's! Surely they'd be able to help!*

Matt reached for the phone and called their office. Rob answered. After a quick exchange of hellos, Matt got down to the reason he'd called.

"Rob, can you take me to Scripps Green in the

morning? I gotta get a check up there, and they told me I would need somebody to take me."

"Ah, Matt, we'd love to! Unfortunately, the two of us are both in surgery tomorrow morning. However . . . what about our daughter, Karlie? You remember her? She'll be home. She can take you!"

"Yeah, Karlie's great! That would be fantastic, Rob. Seriously, thank you so much."

"When do you need her to pick you up?"

"8:30 works."

"8:30 it is! She'll see you then!"

Karlie was at Matt's home bright and early the next morning. She was a very pleasant young lady, who worked in Seattle for a business firm. While he had not met her officially, the two had talked on several occasions while she was in town visiting her parents. After the introductions, they headed off to the hospital. Matt arrived ten minutes prior to his scheduled appointment. Jessica, one of the nurses, was waiting for him. She escorted Sweetwater to the outpatient surgical center, and before they left, she told Karlie that she would be able to pick Matt up in a couple of hours.

The O.R. nurses assisted Jessica in getting Matt ready for the procedure. Within ten minutes, Dr. Rubenson walked in and introduced himself along with his PA (Physician Assistant) Sara, who would assist him with the procedure. Dr. Rubenson was a very distinguished looking man, with a wide friendly smile and a bronze tanned face. Matt immediately liked his bedside manner and professional ethics.

"Okay Matt, here's what I'm going to do. Dr. Abbo mentioned that she heard some irregularities with your heart beat. I'm going to perform a Transesophageal Echocardiogram to get a better look at what's going on with your heart. I'm going to guide a flexible probe down your throat and into your esophagus (the passage leading from your mouth to your stomach). Because the esophagus is located directly behind the heart, it will allow me to scan very close to your heart and get more detailed pictures of your heart beating and direction of blood flow. Once I see what is going on, I'll be able to diagnose your condition. This procedure will only take ten minutes or so, once you're fully sedated. Do you have any questions?"

"No sir, let's get on with it."

"Okay then, Dr. Henricksen will begin administrating the anesthesia and I'll talk with you once the procedure has been completed."

"See you on the other side, doc!"

The next thing Matt remembered was Nurse Jessica holding his hand. Once he was stable and able to comprehend things, he was escorted into Dr. Rubenson's examining room. Within five minutes, the doctor entered the room pulling a TV monitor. Before he proceeded, he asked Matt how he was feeling.

"A little fuzzy doc, but other than that I'm okay."

Once the TV monitor was set up, Dr. Rubenson got right to the point. "Matt, your chordae tendineae has ruptured. These are the special cords of tendon that anchor the mitral valve to the muscles in the bottom chamber of your heart where the blood gets pumped out to the rest of your body. The cords have a tough job to do with every heartbeat."

"That . . . is that serious?"

"It is. Imagine a spring on a door that is broken, and the door doesn't shut completely. That's what is happening here, your mitral valve is not closing properly and you're getting a backflow of blood into your left ventricle, which, if left unrepaired, would lead to congestive heart failure.

"Truth be told, you're a lucky man that Dr. Eva detected this during her exam. It takes a trained ear to pick up something like this."

"Congestive heart failure . . ." Matt said. "So, what does it mean?"

"Well Matt, it means we're going to have to have open heart surgery in order to repair the chordae tendineae."

"Open Heart Surgery? Shit . . . how did this happen? A birth defect? Genetics?"

"No Matt, I don't think so. This is a deceleration type of injury. Normally, we see this kind of thing from sporting accidents, but from your career . . . the sudden stops during carrier landings, the G-forces on your body, and especially with the plane ejection you just had; there's no doubt that this was the straw that broke the camel's back, to be frank with you."

"Is this . . . repairable?" Matt asked with concern.

"Absolutely. Even though I haven't seen the chordae tendineae torn like this before, we have the best cardiac team in the country that will be working on you. We'll fix you up, good as new."

"When are you planning on doing the surgery? The sooner the better, right?"

"Well, we need you rested up, so, for the next four weeks we're going to be running a few tests, but our goal is January 9th."

"Okay doc. Let's get-r-done."

"Good to hear. I'd like for you to see Dr. Jeff Tyner on Monday, he'll be the thoracic surgeon assisting me during your surgery. I'll call the lab and have you scheduled for the work-ups next week."

"Thank you, Doctor."

"Matt, I want you to take it easy over these next few weeks. You'll need to get your energy back and once you do, we'll make you feel like new."

"Yes sir," Sweetwater said, as the doctor departed the examining room.

Jessica entered a few minutes later and escorted Matt to the waiting room where Karlie was waiting to take him home. As they were walking to the car, she enthusiastically asked how things went.

"Not so well, sweetheart . . . Doc said, I have to have Open Heart Surgery."

"Oh my God," she replied, as she gripped his arm.

Once home, Karlie wanted to stay for a while to make sure that Matt was okay. However, he told her that he needed time to comprehend what had been told to him, and that he wanted to be alone. Karlie left as Matt sat in his leather chair, dumbfounded.

For Matt, the next four weeks before the surgery went by like a blur. He notified all concerned parties and got his personal affairs in order. *I could die on that operating table,* he thought to himself. Aside from that, all that Sweetwater had to keep him company for those four weeks were the nurses who drew his blood and stockpiled it, in case of an emergency during surgery, and his own thoughts.

Maybe I should call Mary. She'd like to know, wouldn't she? I shouldn't, though. What kind of an idiot would say, "Hey, I might die. Come be with me." No . . . I can't. If I make it, I'll tell her. I don't want her to worry.

The day of reckoning was quickly approaching, but Matt's fears were lessened when Dr. Tyner, during a checkup, said to him, "Sweetwater, this is a *major routine* surgery; we've got your six covered. Don't you worry about a thing, Gunslinger."

When the day of surgery arrived, Matt found himself in a room surrounded by the Flintom's, his sister Mary Ellen, a surgical nurse, who had flown all the way from Maine to be with him, and a priest, who was about to administer the sacrament of the sick, better known as the Last Rites. *Damn,* Matt thought to himself, *as if this wasn't already creepy enough!* The last thing Matt remembered was Dr. Rubenson's voice, "It's alright Matt—we're just putting you to sleep. We'll see you in a few . . ." And then, darkness.

Eight and a half hours later (and specifically, four hours of being disconnected from his own heart) Matt "Sweetwater" Sullivan opened his eyes. He could see several silhouettes standing next to his bed.

"Oh, he's opening his eyes!" One voice said,

"He's awake! He's awake!" said another.

"How are you feeling, Captain Sullivan?"

Matt tried to answer, but his mouth was too dry to talk. He motioned for some water, to which Donna

Kukura, the head nurse said, "it will be a little longer before you're able to have some crushed ice. Captain, you have some visitors that came to see you." Matt tried intently to figure out who all was there, but everything was still too blurry. "Do you know who these people are?" Donna asked. A face leaned in.

"Matt? Matt? Do you know who I am?"

Matt easily recognized that voice. "Mary . . . is that you?" he weakly mumbled.

"My God Matt, why didn't you get in touch with me? I couldn't believe my eyes when I saw your name on the surgery list this morning!"

"Damn, right out of surgery and he's already in trouble!" one of the mystery voices said.

"Mary, you're still as pretty as ever. Would you like to dance?" Matt said, still feeling the effects of the anesthesia. The room broke out in a fit of laughter.

Mary said with a smile, "I'd love to, Matt. But, I don't think you're quite ready for that yet."

Donna Kukura laughed. "Even after just coming out of open heart surgery, you're still a ladies man, Captain Sullivan." She turned to Mary, "You hold on to this one. He's a keeper."

"Glad to see you made it through, Sweetwater." Another face had leaned in. Matt focused, and then he saw who it was. "Agent Craig Miller!" Matt said, his voice getting stronger. "Goddamn it's good to see you. It's been a long time. How was Iran?"

"Oh, you know. Same shit, different day." The two men laughed. "Listen Captain, you saved our lives back there. You and Johnson both, actually. Buck and I were in some pretty deep shit, but that CHAMP missile and those bombs helped us turn the tide. Seriously, Captain, thank you."

"That's no problem, Bastos. That's what the Gunslingers are trained to do—save guys' asses." The room laughed again.

"Alright, it's my turn now!" It was Gunny Buck Cassidy.

"Well, Buck. Glad to see you didn't miss!"

"No, sir, I sure didn't, right between the running lights, as planned." Matt gave him a thumbs up; for a mission well done."

"So what's changed? Did we really make a difference?" Matt asked.

"Looks that way. Iran has completely backed down from their aspirations of becoming a nuclear power. Rumor has it that they sent President Fletcher a FLASH message that read, 'Message received, loud and clear'."

"Shit hot!" Matt said, trying to clap his hands together. "Sounds like we got 'em then."

"We sure did."

"Really glad to see you made it out safely."

"You, too, Captain. You, too."

Doctor Rubenson entered the room. "Captain Sullivan, how are you feeling?"

"Doc, I feel like I've been speed slapped with a baseball bat."

"Well, that's good, because you kinda look like you have!" Everyone in the room laughed at that.

"Actually doc, I feel like a million bucks after the great news I just received."

"Then I'm going to give you some more good news:

Matt, your chart looks fantastic. Vitals are up, everything looks good. I told you we'd get you through it. Now you just need to get your strength back and grab plenty of rest."

"So, I'm good to go? No more problems?"

"Well, as long as you don't go crashing planes into aircraft carriers anymore, I think we'll be pretty good. Although . . ." Dr. Rubenson said with a pause. "There is someone else who would like to see you."

The doctor motioned towards the door, the charge nurse, Cathie Frost opened the door. "Is he ready?" she asked.

"Yes, please let them come in."

A man, a woman, and a little girl entered the room and walked over to the bed.

"Hello . . ." said Matt. He had no idea who they were.

"Good afternoon, Captain Sullivan, my name is Jason Spangler This is my wife Jennifer, and my daughter, Kaitlynd. I know you don't know us, but we have something that belongs to you, that we'd like to return."

"I don't really know what you're talking about."

Jason looked at Nurse Frost, "Go ahead, please."

Nurse Frost walked outside for a moment and returned with what looked like a big ball of fur on a leash. It didn't take Matt long to realize who it was.

"Boomer! Boomer!" He yelled. Boomer's tail started wagging double-time, and he headed for Matt's bed. It took all of Nurse Frost's strength to keep him on the ground.

"Boomer! Boomer! Boomer!" Matt yelled again in complete surprise. "How in the world did you find my Boomer?"

Matt's blood pressure and vitals started to go off the charts, so they had to calm both man and beast down, with Boomer resisting the combined efforts of Jason, his wife Jennifer, his little girl Kaitlynd, and Nurse Frost attempting to keep him from jumping onto the bed. Once the two long-lost friends were calm, Boomer was placed on the bed, and he snuggled up in between Matt's legs. Little Kaitlynd came over and put her arms around Boomer's neck and laid her head against his.

Jennifer and Jason then proceeded to tell the story about how Boomer had wandered into their backyard, bruised and bloodied one afternoon while Kaitlynd was playing in her sandbox.

"When I walked out there at first," Jason said, "I was terrified. Boomer dwarfed her, obviously, but he had such a presence of peace. Kaitlynd was rubbing his face, and I noticed that he had a large porcupine quill stuck in his nose. We quickly loaded Boomer up into the car, took him to the vet, and got it removed."

"After that, we basically adopted Boomer as our own. We didn't think anything of it until we saw the notices . . . we put two and two together, and then we began to search for you. It was a blessing that we could reunite both of you today. We're so very glad that we could bring your buddy back to you, though," he said.

Kaitlynd kissed Boomer on the head and said, "Bye bye, Boomer. I love you." Tears started running down Matt's cheek as he said, "I knew you would always come back to me, Boomerang."

ABOUT THE AUTHOR

WILLIAM H. LaBARGE is a twenty-three-year Navy Carrier Pilot Veteran, with many of those years working for SOG (special operation group). LaBarge retired as a Commercial Airline Pilot after twenty years and is a member of the Writers Guild of America. He is the National Bestselling Author of Aviation Book of the Year *Sweetwater Gunslinger 201*, along with *Hornets Nest*, *Road to Gold*, and *Desert Voices*. He served as a technical advisor for the movies *Final Countdown*, *Top Gun*, *Firefox*, and the TV series *JAG*. Bill and his wife live in California for more information on William LaBarge you can visit his web site: www.WilliamLaBarge.com

CPSIA information can be obtained at www.ICGtesting.com
Printed in the USA
LVOW05s1336271213

367086LV00001B/3/P